C000182434

ONE KISS FOR CHRISTMAS

MICHELE BROUDER

Editing by Jessica Peirce

Book Cover Design by Michelle Arzu, www.mnarzuauthor.com

Formatting by www.madcatdesigns.net

One Kiss For Christmas

ISBN-10: 9781709896309

To God be the Glory.

In memory of my grandmother,
Ruth Zimmer

PROLOGUE

 ctober

DONNA ST. JAMES drove away from the airport Sunday morning, looking forward to getting home. Tanned and relaxed, she was pleased with her decision to tack a week of vacation onto the five-day conference in Florida she'd been required to attend for her job as a financial advisor at the bank. The sunshine and heat had been hard to beat, and her joints thanked her, although she had to admit to looking forward to autumn in her hometown of Orchard Falls in upstate New York. She blasted the heater in her car to ward off the chillier weather that had greeted her as soon as she stepped off the plane.

Before going back to the house, she thought she'd make one quick stop at the grocery store to pick up the newspaper and her favorite Danish. She was able to snag a parking spot on Main Street right in front of the shop. Fallen leaves crunched beneath her feet on the sidewalk as she headed into the store. From a distance, she saw some friends from her knitting group and waved to them.

The intoxicating smell of baked goods hit her as soon as she stepped through the automatic doors of Gunderman's grocery store. Donna curled a newspaper under one arm and made her way through the usual Sunday customers and over to the bakery, where she used the stainless-steel tongs to stuff one cheese Danish into a waxy, brown paper bag.

With her items in hand, Donna headed toward the cash registers. Waiting for her at the only open checkout was Sarge, a lifelong employee. Sarge had worked at Gunderman's for as long as Donna could remember. And she had not changed much in over three decades. There were two notable features about Sarge: her short, tight set of curls and her miserable personality. Donna had never once seen her smile. Her real name was Marge, but she'd been dubbed "Sarge" early on and it had stuck.

"Good morning, Sarge," Donna said, laying her items on the belt.

Sarge paused with Donna's newspaper in her hand. "Is it? I mean, it's kind of chilly outside, and nobody is raking up their leaves and they're turning to muck and starting to smell."

"I know," Donna said. She'd learned a long time ago that there was no sense in protesting or voicing a different opinion to Sarge's. It would just set her off and hold up the line. The last thing Donna wanted to do was get on Sarge's bad side but unfortunately, Donna had yet to see a good side. She was hopeful though.

Sarge lifted the bakery bag and stared at Donna as if she were a TSA employee and this were the airport. "What's in the bag?" she demanded, like she did every Sunday morning.

"One cheese Danish," Donna replied, giving her standard weekly answer. She stopped short of saluting.

Sarge regarded her for a moment and then opened up the bag.

"Store policy. I have to look in the bag." Donna rolled her eyes. *Why does she always ask what's inside when she's going to look anyway?*

Checking out was always like a test you knew you were going to fail, or an answer you didn't have for the teacher no matter how much you'd prepared, Donna thought.

Once cashed out, she headed back home, taking her time, driving slowly. Her plans for a lazy Sunday were to make a big pot of chili and watch the football game with her son, Brent. He'd said he'd pick up some apple cider from Walmott's Farm just outside of town. The suitcase and the laundry could wait. By Donna's calendar, she was still on vacation.

Donna had lived in Orchard Falls her whole life and there wasn't any place she'd rather be. On Main Street she passed the town's only movie house with its marquee of red and gold lights. Across the street from that was the old five-and-dime with its green and white striped awning. But her favorite landmark was the old, red milk machine at the corner of Main and Monroe. It no longer dispensed quarts of milk but it stood there as a testament to the past. There was the three-story dark-red brick Benjamin Franklin High School she had attended like her parents and grandparents before her, and then the commercial part of Main Street transitioned to private homes: grand old Victorians and farmhouses with gingerbread trim, big front lawns, and wide sidewalks.

Donna's house was situated three blocks from the grocery store, on Cherry Street, which ran parallel to Main Street. There was a nice variety of old Victorian, brick, mission-style, and farmhouse-style homes. It as was an eclectic mix but it worked. It gave the area character.

When she pulled into her driveway, she put her car in park and frowned. Her favorite tree, a Norway maple that towered over her backyard, looked oddly different. Leaving her groceries in the car, she headed up the driveway to get a better look. Once the entire tree came into view, Donna gasped. Some of the branches that had previously hung over the neighboring fence were gone. On one side, the tree had been stripped bare, disfiguring it.

Her temper rising, she glanced at the house next door and saw an SUV in the driveway. Her former neighbor, Mrs. Patton, had died back in the spring. The house had been sold at the end of the summer and the rumor circulating was that it had been purchased by a retiree. The new owner must have moved in while she was gone. And sawed off the branches of her favorite tree!

"Oh!" she said. Furious, she marched across the thin strip of lawn that separated her driveway from the neighboring one.

She banged on the side door. It was when she was on the second round of banging against the storm door that a figure appeared behind the glass.

A tall, solid man opened the door. Donna, still irate, launched into her tirade. "What happened to my tree? Who cut off the branches? Did you do this?"

Donna stopped, her eyes widening and her mouth falling open as she looked at her new neighbor. She'd know those blazing blue eyes anywhere. Even after all this time. Her breath caught in her throat.

The man spoke first, seemingly impervious to her outburst. "Donna? Donna Van Dyke?" he asked, incredulous, using her maiden name, a surname she hadn't used in almost three decades.

Jim "Big Jim" O'Hara looked almost the same as he had when he and Donna dated during high school and college. All those years in the military had left him chiseled, but his dark hair had now gone silver. His eyes were still a brilliant shade of blue. Donna's mother used to say he had Paul Newman eyes.

Donna swallowed hard as the past came calling. "What are you doing here?" she asked, her voice shaking.

"I live here," he replied.

"You bought Mrs. Patton's house?" she asked, wondering about the cruel cosmic joke that was being played on her.

"I did. Retired from the Army after thirty years and my plan had always been to come back to Orchard Falls."

Donna didn't say anything. She didn't know what to say or where to begin. Her former high-school sweetheart was now her next-door neighbor? How could that be?

"You look great, Donna," he said softly.

She felt her cheeks flush in a way that had nothing to do with the change of life. She looked at her tree. "Too bad you can't say the same thing about my tree," she said, unable to keep the edge out of her voice. She folded her arms across her chest to ward off the chill. The sunshine was warm but weak.

"The leaves are all over my backyard. I didn't retire to spend my days raking up leaves from somebody else's tree," he explained.

"So, you just start sawing off branches without letting me know?" she asked, her voice rising. "Without asking permission?"

"I left several notes in your mailbox," he said.

"I've been gone for two weeks!" she said.

Jim appeared uneasy. He scratched the back of his head. "I am sorry, Donna," he said. "Why don't you come in and have a cup of coffee."

Donna shook her head. "Uh, no thanks. I've got a butchered tree to tend to." Bitterness crept into her voice.

"It's just a little trim," he said.

"Just a little trim?" Donna repeated in disbelief. She shook her head and eyed her misshapen tree. "That's enough cutting. No more."

"As long as you rake any leaves that fall on my property," he said, putting his hands on his hips. He used to do that a lot, back in the day. When he was feeling confident. Sure of himself. Three decades ago, she'd found it attractive. Today that stance irritated her. Funny how she'd remembered, though.

"Sure, no problem," she said, and she turned on her heel and headed back home with him behind her, watching.

Donna shook inside. The last time she'd seen Jim was Christmas 1990, when he'd dumped her and broken her heart.

CHAPTER 1

*N*ovember

THE LAST SATURDAY BEFORE THANKSGIVING, everyone in town had the same idea: get a carton of the limited-edition candy cane ice cream that the Orchard Falls Dairy only put out at Christmastime. Donna ignored her shopping list, heading straight to the freezer section to get her carton. She waited all year for this. It was like the first snowfall. As she turned down the aisle, she saw Jim O'Hara wheeling his cart down the neighboring aisle. Wearing reading glasses, he scrutinized his list, not seeing her. Thank God for small favors, she thought. Since their confrontation last month, she'd caught glimpses of him coming and going from next door. And a few times, she'd ducked down from her kitchen window after catching him glancing at her house.

Arriving at the ice cream section, she scanned the selection and her shoulders sagged. She scrunched up her nose. No sign of candy cane ice cream. The entire shelf was empty.

Sarge walked by, pushing a cart of boxed ice cream cakes.

"Hey, Sarge, any chance there's more candy cane ice cream in the back?" Donna inquired. The expression on Sarge's face made Donna regret asking.

"Yeah, Donna, because it's so popular we keep it all in the back," Sarge answered, scowling. "The store has no interest in making a profit."

Donna waited, knowing Sarge was by no means finished. She was just warming up. "I can tell you exactly what's in the back, from the twelve pallets of Pepsi to the twenty-five crates of two percent milk to the all the leftover pumpkin-spice cupcakes that are going on markdown tomorrow."

Donna didn't doubt Sarge knew the complete contents of the back room.

"Okay, thanks anyway," Donna muttered, pushing her cart away. She sighed and decided she'd try again the next day. But her eye was caught by the small, portable freezer case at the end of the aisle. There was a sign that read "Candy Cane Ice Cream." She pushed her cart at breakneck speed, glad for all the walking and yoga she did. As she arrived at the case, her cart banged into another cart, but she ignored it as she looked into the freezer case. In the corner, at the bottom, was the last carton of ice cream, all bedecked with its trademark red and white stripes. Just looking for a new home.

As Donna reached for it, so did another, bigger arm. Her hand closed around the carton at the same time another, bigger hand did. She recognized the familiar college class ring and she didn't look up to see who the arm belonged to. She didn't have to.

Jim O'Hara.

Despite this, she didn't let go. But neither did he.

They both held onto the carton and stood up, drawing it out of the freezer case and staring at each other.

"I believe this is mine," she said sweetly.

He shook his head, his silver hair still cut short, military style. "I don't think so, Donna."

"So much for gallantry and ladies first," she huffed.

He laughed. "Are you kidding? I'd knock down old ladies and steal kids' lunch money for a pint of this stuff," he said. "I haven't had it in over three decades."

"Whose fault is that?" she asked, wishing she hadn't sounded so sharp. It made her seem bitter about how things turned out between them, which she wasn't.

"It's one of the things I've been looking forward to since I returned to Orchard Falls."

This statement only served to irritate her more, and she held on tighter.

"Now, children, don't fight," said a voice from behind them. Donna recognized it as belonging to her best friend, Christine Horst. They'd been friends since the third grade.

"Fine, have it." Jim sighed, letting go of the ice cream. "But you owe me."

Donna shot him a warning look and turned to Christine. "Hi, Christine," Donna said.

"Is that Christine Amalfi?" Jim asked.

"It's Christine Horst now," Donna said, nodding. "Chris, you remember Jim O'Hara?" Donna didn't relay the fact that after she'd discovered he was her new neighbor, she'd called her best friend immediately.

Christine wore her brown hair short with highlights of cinnamon and honey, and flicking in all directions. Christine leaned in and gave Jim a hug. "No way! Wow, how long has it been?"

"Almost thirty years?" Jim ventured. "How are you, Christine?"

"I'm well," Christine answered. "I married Eugene right out of college and we're still together."

9

"That's terrific. Kids?"

"Oh yeah. A slew of them. Six kids," Christine replied. With a laugh, she added, "I haven't had any peace and quiet since 1993."

Jim laughed along with her.

Christine turned back to Donna. "Don't forget the committee meeting for the Snowball Festival on Tuesday night."

"Is that still going on?" Jim asked with a grin.

"It is," Christine replied. She looked slyly from Donna to Jim. "You should join a committee."

Donna widened her eyes at Christine as if to say, "What do you think you're doing?"

"I might just do that," Jim said. "I'm looking for things to do since I retired."

"Any of the committees would love the help," Christine said. "Look, I've got to go. It was good seeing you, Jim." They hugged again and as she walked away, she looked at Donna with an exaggerated expression and told her she'd call her.

Donna nodded. Christine had gotten full-body contact, and all she'd gotten was a few sawn-off tree limbs. Sighing, she looked at the lone carton of ice cream in the corner of her cart.

Jim laughed. "It was good seeing you again, Donna." He nodded toward the ice cream. "Don't forget you owe me for that." He smiled at her. The straight white teeth, the strong jawline, those hypnotic blue eyes—Donna's heart rate entered into a territory that was dangerous for people her age. She wanted to crawl into the freezer case to cool off.

Quickly, she pulled the carton of ice cream out of her cart and handed it to him. The last thing she wanted was to be indebted to Jim O'Hara. "Here, take this, then."

He laughed and put up his hand, refusing it. "You keep it."

"What do you want?" she said, sounding brusque. They were no longer back in high school, and she wasn't going to be coy. And there would be no flirting!

He took hold of his cart and winked at her. "I'll need to think about this. I'll get back to you and let you know." He pushed his cart off, whistling along with the Christmas music coming from the store's overhead intercom.

Donna just stood there, staring after him, her candy cane ice cream melting in her cart.

CHAPTER 2

*J*im stood in his kitchen, talking on the phone to his daughter, Leah.

"I'd love for you to come and spend Christmas here with me, honey," Jim said, walking over to the sink to look out the window. His kitchen window overlooked his driveway and Donna's house on the other side of it.

The phone just about reached the window. It was a wall phone left by the previous owner, and its long spiral cord coiled to the floor. The color: harvest gold. It was such a throwback to his childhood that he had no plans to replace it.

"I'll see, Dad," Leah replied.

More than anything, Jim would love for his only child to spend Christmas with him in Orchard Falls. Especially as he navigated the new adventure of retirement. When he'd first arrived in October, he'd been busy with the house: painting the interior, fixing a leak in the kitchen, and refinishing some of the hardwood floors. He could have hired someone to do the work but he'd needed something to do with all his free time. He'd pulled out the half-dead shrubs in front of the porch and replaced them with bulbs for the spring. But after almost six weeks, the inside and the outside of the house were where he wanted them to be. And now with the long winter looming ahead of him, he felt a restlessness beginning to take hold.

"Were you thinking about going to your mother's?" he asked, referring to his ex-wife, Carol. They'd divorced when Leah was four but had remained on somewhat friendly terms. She had not been interested in being a military wife. And he'd only been interested in his career in the military.

"No, she and Pete are going to Florida for the holiday," Leah answered.

"And you don't want to go with Mom and your stepdad?" he asked, pacing around the kitchen as he talked.

"Ew, don't call him that. He's just Pete," Leah protested. Jim could almost see her scrunching up her nose like she used to do when she was twelve.

"But he is your stepfather," Jim pointed out. He opened up a cupboard door, rooting around for a snack.

"Yeah, but I'm too old to think of him that way," Leah said.

Jim remembered when he was in his twenties. He'd felt he could take on the world. He still felt that way, just maybe not as fast, or in smaller increments.

"Come on, it's Christmas, you should spend it with one of your parents," Jim said. Finally deciding on pretzels, he pulled out a bag.

"I'll probably come to Orchard Falls," she said. "I'd be interested in seeing your hometown."

"Good. What fence are you chaining yourself to this week?" he asked.

"Dad!" she said, sounding bored. "Actually, we're protesting at a cosmetics company. Animal testing and stuff, you know."

"Yeah, I know," he answered. And he did. Leah had loved animals since she was a little girl, and Carol had allowed her the usual bevy of pets: fish, hamsters, birds, cats, and dogs. And Leah had traveled with all her successive pets when spending her summers or holidays with Jim, which had thrilled him to no end. When Leah was thirteen, she announced she was going vegan, and he and Carol spent many a late night on the phone figuring out the best way to deal with it and make sure that at the same time, Leah ate a nutritious diet. Since then, his daughter had never wavered in her commitment to animals. He couldn't help but admire that and feel that he and Carol had done something right by her, despite their divorce.

"Just be careful," Jim said, munching on a pretzel.

"I will," Leah said. "What are you eating?"

"Pretzels."

"Can I bring the cats with me?"

"Do I have a choice?" he asked. He wasn't a big fan of cats. And her cats were weird.

She laughed. "I've got to go, But I'll let you know my plans as soon as I know them."

"Okay, Leah, talk soon," he said and hung up.

He walked back over to the sink and poured a glass of water from the tap. Donna exiting her house caught his eye. Of all the people in the world, he couldn't believe he'd ended up living next door to Donna Van Dyke. After some discreet inquiries, he'd learned that she was now Donna St. James, a widow with one grown son. She'd never left Orchard Falls. Even back in high school, she'd never expressed any interest in leaving Orchard Falls, spreading her wings and seeing the world. She looked great. Like him, she'd aged, but her hair was still a beautiful shade of auburn and her eyes a clear, sharp green.

The other day down at Gunderman's had been unexpected and fun. Things hadn't changed, and it made him both relieved and nostalgic. The shop had definitely not plowed their profit back into the store. And Sarge, the perennial employee, was still as cranky as ever. He was glad to see that Donna and Christine were still friends after all these years. He hoped she was enjoying that carton of candy cane ice cream; she owed him bigtime.

The fact that Donna lived next door certainly made things interesting. But he'd hardly seen her since that confrontation about cutting down her tree. And he preferred it that way. Donna St. James was a lot of things. But for him, she'd be forever labeled as the one who got away.

THE FOLLOWING MORNING, Jim went to the Main Street Diner for breakfast. A former trolley car, it had been converted to a restaurant that only did breakfast and lunch. There were small booths that seated up to four, and a Formica lunch counter in front lined with vinyl-padded stools. The place smelled of freshly brewed coffee, bacon, and frying onions. There were the usual sounds of clattering dishes and clinking spoons and the hum of conversation among the diners.

Jim's dad used to bring him in on Saturday mornings for a stack of pancakes. Not much had changed there, either. Christmas decorations of gold garland, lights, and red ornaments gave it a merry atmosphere. He stomped his boots on the winter mat, shaking the snow off of them, and scanned the area. From a back booth, he saw the hand of Steve Perez wave to him. With a nod, he headed back to join his old friend.

Steve stood up from the booth and broke into a wide smile. "Jim! How's it going?"

"Good."

They each slid into a side of the booth. He and Steve had been good friends since grammar school. His friend's dark eyes were the same, but his black hair had departed the top of his head, and what was left on the sides was now white. Although Jim had left the area almost three decades ago, they'd always kept in touch, usually via email and Christmas cards.

Steve owned the optical place next door to the old cinema. When Jim had first retired, he'd reached out to Steve, expressing an interest in returning to Orchard Falls. His friend had been encouraging and had even introduced him to a real estate agent. Lately they'd been meeting every Monday morning for breakfast before Steve opened his optical office.

"How's retirement going?" Steve asked after they placed their orders.

Jim shrugged, sighing. "It's been an adjustment. I'm not used to doing nothing. And I'm not used to quiet, small-town life."

"Are you regretting moving back here?" Steve asked, sipping his coffee.

"Not yet," Jim said. He drank his coffee black. "When I left for college, I always felt that someday, I'd make my way back here. I always wanted to end back up in my hometown, but now I'm wondering if the place may be too sedate for me. It never is how you remember it, is it?" He paused and took a sip of his coffee.

"I guess not."

"I'm going to give it some time and if it's not for me, I'll move someplace else, maybe closer to Leah, if she ever settles down."

"How old is she now?"

"Just turned twenty-five. Training guide dogs for the blind. Animal-rights activist," Jim said. "She might be visiting at Christmas. She's also a dedicated vegan, so there'll be no steaks for me while she's here."

"Ouch," Steve said with a laugh.

"How are Lynn and the kids?" Jim asked.

"Fine. Actually, Kyle is thinking of joining one of the

branches of the service after graduation and I was wondering if you would talk to him," Steve said.

"Not a problem. Stop over any time," Jim said.

The server interrupted them, setting their breakfasts down in front of them. Jim had a stack of pancakes and a side plate of bacon, crisp.

Jim covered his stack with butter and maple syrup and after the first bite said, "Donna Van Dyke is my next-door neighbor."

Steve's fork paused midair and he asked, "Who? What?"

"Donna Van Dyke . . . er . . . Donna St. James."

Steve's eyes widened. "No, really?" He processed the idea and added with a raised eyebrow, "That should be interesting."

"I'm beginning to wonder."

"Any chance you two might get back together?" Steve asked.

Without hesitation, Jim replied, "Oh no, that's in the past."

Steve shook his head and laughed. "You living next door to Donna. Now that's hilarious."

"I'm sure she thinks so too," Jim said. He wondered what she thought about it. Actually, he wasn't sure what he thought about it himself. Of all the houses he could buy in the world, he'd gone and bought the one next to his favorite old flame.

"When we were in high school, everyone—and I mean everyone—thought you two would definitely end up together," Steve said. "It was like a sure thing."

"Yeah, that's what we thought as well," Jim said.

He and Donna had dated the last two years of high school and through college. But there'd been that little thing about him going away to college and then off to serve in Iraq back in '91. The relationship had derailed that Christmas, before the start of Desert Storm.

Steve turned the subject to sports, namely football and hockey, and Jim went along with him, but thoughts of Donna lingered at the back of his mind, along with the question of what might have been.

—————

As Christine had mentioned, Jim spotted a notice in the *Orchard Falls Gazette* about a committee meeting for the Snowball Festival. In an effort to keep boredom at bay, he figured he might as well go and see what was going on. It was scheduled for seven in the community center. He wondered if Donna would be there. He thought briefly of asking her to drive with him, but then thought better of it. Since he'd moved in, he'd hardly seen her. He couldn't help but wonder if that was deliberate on her part.

Jim was used to being busy. He wasn't keen to end up as a channel surfer on the sofa. You sit, you die, was his motto. And no matter where he'd lived, whether in the US or abroad, he'd always gotten involved in the local community. It had been important for him to give Leah a sense of community that extended past the military families.

The Orchard Falls Community Center was located between the village hall and the fire department. He parked his SUV in the lot behind the building. As he headed around to the front, he noticed Donna walking ahead of him, treading carefully over the light dusting of snow covering the sidewalk. Even after all these years, he knew the sight of her, the shape of her. The way she walked. It was something that had been ingrained in his mind when he was a teenager.

She wore a knit hat pulled down over her head with only wisps of her auburn hair peeking out. She wore a plum-colored ski jacket and a pair of jeans.

Jim followed her inside, wondering if there would ever be closure to what had transpired between them all those years ago.

He felt he at least deserved an explanation for what had happened. Or more specifically, what hadn't happened.

The community center was packed and this surprised him. He immediately recognized Steve and waved. There were only a few empty seats left and he had no choice but to sit down next to Donna with a nod and a smile. He saw Sarge, Ralph, and Christine in the row ahead of them but didn't immediately recognize anyone else.

A tall woman with a sharp, blunt-angled cut of blonde hair took the stage. She wore a Christmas sweater with a pair of jeans.

Jim leaned forward in his chair and narrowed his eyes at the familiar face on stage.

"Is that Mary Ellen Schumacher?" he whispered to Donna, leaning closer to make himself heard. He could smell her perfume, something nice and soft.

"It is," Donna replied, not looking at him. Mary Ellen Schumacher had been the head cheerleader in high school, the all-around student: great grades and active in a lot of after-school clubs.

"What's she doing now?" he asked.

"She has a dental practice here in town," Donna said.

"Good for her," Jim said. "She looks like a dentist."

Donna turned to face him, leveling her gaze at him. "What does a dentist look like?"

Jim shrugged. Why did she have the power, after all this time, to discombobulate him and have him tripping over his words? "I don't know. Like someone you trust to put their hands into your mouth?"

Donna snorted, which made Jim laugh, but she quickly recovered and her mask of indifference fell back into place.

"Did she ever get married?" he asked, curious.

Donna shook her head. "No, probably too busy with all the clubs and meetings she runs."

Mary Ellen stepped up to the podium and adjusted the mic.

"Just like high school," Jim added.

"Shh," Donna said.

Mary Ellen called the meeting to order with a smile. "It's great to see such a large turnout. Let's make this our best Snowball Festival ever!" she said, rallying the crowd.

Once the clapping and hooting settled down, she said, "As most of you know, I'm in charge of the overall festival, which takes place the weekend before Christmas. We'll follow the same schedule as we have for years. On Friday, we'll kick off with outdoor activities like ice skating and outdoor hockey and end the night with toboggan races. Saturday is the craft fair, and we have the grade-school coloring contest. Saturday evening is the talent show and of course, Sunday evening is the dance. There are the usual committees: entertainment, outdoor activities, decorations, safety and many more." Her gaze swept the room and she added, "It looks like we'll have plenty of people."

Jim glanced around the meeting room, noting some familiar faces from his past. Like him, they'd either gotten grayer or heavier.

"Okay, can I have everyone's attention, please?" Mary Ellen said. There was a still a buzz coursing through the room, and people kept talking. Mary Ellen laughed and raised her voice. "Hey, listen up! Let's get started here."

In front of Jim, Sarge muttered. "Yeah, let's get started. Let's not make this our life's work."

"All right, we need to start by selecting the head of each committee. From there I'll assign volunteers."

There were a couple of coughs and whispers tittering through the crowd.

"First we need someone to oversee the outside activities committee," Mary Ellen said, glancing around the room. "This person will be in charge of overseeing any activity that happens outside, like ice skating and toboggan races. Any volunteers?"

Jim looked around the room and thought this might be something he could do. Tentatively, he raised his hand. Donna looked in his direction but said nothing, and he shrugged.

Mary Ellen's gaze moved to Jim's raised hand but passed right by him. She turned her attention to Steve.

"Steve, do you think you can handle this?"

"I didn't have my hand raised," Steve protested.

"That's great then, thanks Steve," Mary Ellen said, ignoring his objection. She glanced back at Jim and said to Steve, "I'm sure you'll have no problem getting help."

Jim sat back in his folding wooden chair and sighed. He heard a twitter from Donna.

"Next is the safety committee. This is just what it sounds like: making sure all the roads for the festival are salted, organizing first-aid facilities, fire extinguishers, coordinating with local emergency services, etc., etc. Any volunteers?"

Again, Jim's hand was the first one up. Mary Ellen looked at him, but her eyes eventually landed on Ray Malinowski, Chief of Police. "Okay, Ray, this one's yours."

"A busman's holiday," joked the chief, and everyone laughed.

Jim wondered why he was being ignored. He'd never thought of Orchard Falls as a closed community. Maybe he'd been gone too long and was now viewed as an outsider.

Mary Ellen assigned the decorations committee to Donna. She then asked for volunteers for the various committees. Jim refrained from volunteering. For Donna's committee, Mary Ellen immediately picked Sarge and Christine when they raised their hands. Looking around the community center, she asked, "Can we have some men for a change, as well?"

Sarge elbowed her husband, Ralph, who tentatively raised his hand.

"Thanks, Ralph, that's great. One more fella. Come on, guys," Mary Ellen pleaded with a laugh.

Jim did not raise his hand. He had nothing against decorations, but he had no interest in working side by side with Donna.

"What about you there?" Mary Ellen said into her mic.

Jim pretended he didn't see her staring straight at him. He lowered his head.

"The guy sitting next to Donna," Mary Ellen clarified.

Jim's head shot up. "Me?" he mouthed.

Mary Ellen laughed. "Yes, you. What's your name?"

"Jim O'Hara," he said quietly.

There was a murmuring in the crowd as heads turned toward him. Beside him, Donna lowered her head and coughed.

"Big Jim?" Mary Ellen asked, her face breaking into a smile of recognition. "Why didn't you say so? I had no idea who you were earlier."

Jim gave her a hapless smile.

"Consider yourself chosen for Donna's committee," she said with a grin.

Before he could protest, Mary Ellen moved on to the next order of business.

After the meeting, nearly everyone lingered at the back of the hall over coffee, tea, and Christmas cookies. A lot of people approached Jim, welcoming him back to Orchard Falls.

As he reminisced with people, he was aware of Donna on the periphery, sipping a cup of coffee. When he was finally alone, he skipped another cup of coffee, because he didn't want to be up all night. But he did help himself to another Christmas cookie.

Donna approached him.

"Look, Jim, you don't have to be on the committee," she started. "I'm sure we'll manage without you." Her expression was unreadable.

Something about her dismissive tone rankled him, and

suddenly there wasn't anything more he wanted to do than decorate, a pastime he usually didn't cherish. "I'd like to join you on the decorations committee," he said.

She didn't hide her surprise. "Really?"

He nodded. "Yes. Why does that surprise you?"

She shrugged. "I just didn't think a veteran of a tour of duty would be interested in 'decorations.'" She added her own air quotes.

He didn't correct her and say that he had done a total of three tours of duty. The first back in '91 and then two more in Iraq and Afghanistan after 9-11. Instead, he said, "Does decorating a canteen for Christmas in Afghanistan count?"

She laughed, her smile reaching her eyes, and he relaxed.

"It sure does," she said. "I'll take you on my team."

An uncomfortable silence fell between them. There were fine lines around her eyes and mouth, but to him, she was still beautiful. Her eyes were clear and bright. Before he could get too caught up in the old attraction to her again, he reminded himself that all that was over between them. That had been her decision. The final one.

He said a quick goodnight and headed toward the parking lot.

Jim knew he had no business getting involved with Donna again, no matter how attractive he found her. He'd had no luck with personal relationships; from Donna to his ex-wife, he had just been unlucky in love. It wasn't him being down on himself, it was him just stating a fact.

He reminded himself that Donna was his past and too much time had elapsed since then. What he'd wanted at eighteen or twenty wasn't necessarily what he wanted now at fifty-three. Besides, her silence from all those years ago had told him everything he needed to know about what Donna wanted. Or didn't want. Or more specifically, *whom* she didn't want.

CHAPTER 3

ecember

"Mom, are you okay?" Brent asked.

Donna looked up quickly from her knitting at her only child. "I am. Why do you ask?"

"You're kind of quiet tonight," he said. Brent had stopped by after work to bring up her boxes of decorations from the basement, as well as the seven-foot-tall artificial Christmas tree.

She laughed. That was funny coming from him. There was no one quieter than her son. As a child he'd been painfully shy, and he'd grown into a reserved young man. Brent didn't say too much, but he never wasted his words when he did speak.

She smiled at him, reassuring him. "I'm fine. Just thinking about the run-up to the Snowball Festival and everything that needs to be done. The usual."

He nodded but his expression said he wasn't totally convinced.

Donna didn't dare trouble him with her worries about Jim

24

O'Hara. It wasn't Brent's job as her son to give her advice or provide a shoulder for her to cry on. But since the arrival of her former high-school sweetheart, she'd felt as if her world had turned upside down. More than once since October, she'd thought of selling her house and moving somewhere else in Orchard Falls. But why should she move? She'd been there first. She was just going to have to learn to live with it. Make peace with it. Now, if only she could stop staring out her kitchen window trying to get a glimpse of him going or coming into his home. She was a fifty-year-old woman acting like a sixteen-year-old girl.

"Mom?" Brent said. Had he been speaking to her? She hadn't noticed.

"Hmmm, yes?" she asked, focusing all her attention on her son.

With his height and blonde hair, he resembled her late husband. But he had green eyes like his mother.

Brent nodded toward her needlework. "What are you knitting? I think we have enough afghans."

She peered over her cheaters. "Ha ha. One of the things we're doing for this year's festival is yarn bombing everything on Main Street."

"Won't it get wet?" he asked with a frown. Brent was so practical and serious. Just like his father. She wished he'd enjoy his life more. All he did was work, work, work. Just like his father had done—and look what had happened to him.

"Most likely," she said, her needles slipping back into their familiar rhythm. "It will all be taken down after Christmas. But it's something different to do."

He nodded but said nothing.

"I'm going to ask the group if we can wash and donate the items after we take them down," she said.

Brent frowned. "But who could use it?"

Donna's needles halted and she appeared thoughtful. "Maybe you could use them at the clinic? For the cages?"

"Maybe," he said, mulling it over.

Donna frowned and said to herself, "Let me think about this." She resumed her knitting. She looked over at Brent and said, "There's some candy cane ice cream in the freezer."

That got his interest. "Really? My favorite," he said, stepping into the kitchen.

Donna smiled to herself. She wasn't much of a baker, but she always made sure she had plenty of candy cane ice cream on hand. She reminded herself to give Sally Pratt a call and put in her order for Christmas cookies.

"Mom, do you want a bowl?" he called from the kitchen.

"No thanks, Brent, I'll have one later when I'm watching my show," she said.

He reappeared with a generous amount of ice cream in a cereal bowl. He plopped down on the sofa across from her. "What horror show are you watching now?" he asked.

"Usual stuff," she said with a laugh.

"Honestly, Mom, I don't know how you sleep at night," he said, spooning ice cream into his mouth. "I take one look at your list on Netflix and I feel like I need to call an exorcist."

"Oh, Brent." She laughed. "It's not that bad."

"Yeah, Mom, it is," he said.

Changing the subject, she asked, "So, what are your plans for the weekend?"

He shrugged, nonchalant. "The usual. Saturday's a half day at the clinic and I'll probably go to the gym after that. And on Sunday."

Donna worried about her son. Ever since Gloria had dumped him three years back, he seemed to have put his life on hold. When he'd opened his veterinary clinic in town last year, he'd thrown himself into his work. He'd purchased a small starter house and it only had furniture in three rooms. It looked as empty as his life. When she'd commented on the sparsity of it, he'd looked at her, shrugged and asked, "What else do I need?"

Her wish for him was to find someone who was worthy of him. Someone to appreciate his quiet solidness and accept him as he was. He was never going to be the life of the party, but he had many admirable qualities that made her proud. He had so much to offer the right girl. Donna would love to see him settled down with a family of his own.

"So I guess we'll have Christmas dinner here, as usual?" Donna said.

"Just the two of us?" Brent asked.

Donna thought for a moment. "Does that bother you?"

He shook his head and smiled.

"I could invite some people if you'd like," she suggested. At the same time, she racked her brain as to who they could ask over.

Brent chuckled. "Mom, it's fine. It's been the two of us for a long time now."

"It has," she agreed. Once she'd got over the initial shock of widowhood, she'd thrown herself into motherhood, her career, and carving out a life for herself as a single woman. She'd worked hard to raise her son.

Brent went and got himself a second bowl of ice cream. They sat in companionable silence for the rest of the evening until he left. She waved from the driveway as he pulled out. They saw each other a couple times a week and they texted almost every day.

As she headed back into her house, Jim called over from his driveway.

"Donna!" he called out. He parked his wheelie bins, which he'd been taking out to the curb, and trotted over to her, his boots crunching in the snow.

"Hi, Jim," she said.

"When will there be a meeting for the decorations committee?" he asked.

"It's tomorrow night here at my house at seven," she replied.

"When were you going to tell me? Friday morning?" he asked good-naturedly.

"I don't have your number to include you in a group text," she said.

He whipped out his cell phone, pulled off his glove and began swiping. "Give me your number," he said.

She swallowed hard, thinking back to that day in her sophomore year before school let out for summer vacation, when he'd approached her at her locker and said, "Can I call you over the break? Will you give me your number?" She'd been shocked, but secretly pleased.

Coming back from her reverie, she rattled off her number.

When he was finished saving it, he said, "I've sent you mine." And within a second, her phone beeped with an incoming notification.

She nodded. "Okay, thanks." The night air was brisk and Donna could feel her nose threatening to run. She had stepped outside without her jacket.

"Now for tomorrow night, do I need to bring anything?" he asked.

"Just yourself. We do have something to eat so if you wanted to bring a snack or a dessert to pass around, that would be appreciated," she said.

"Will do," he said, and turned to go. Over his shoulder, he called, "I'll see you tomorrow night, Donna."

She watched him as he finished wheeling his bins to the end of his driveway, whistling.

She didn't know what to make of his presence in her life again after all this time. Maybe it didn't have to mean anything, she told herself. And really, after all that had happened, it couldn't mean anything. It wouldn't mean anything, she decided. But then why did she feel as if her life was already altering and she had no control over it?

DONNA DID some last-minute cleaning after work before the arrival of the decorations committee. She turned on the potpourri warmer with a bayberry melt. This wasn't the first time she'd had a meeting at her house. But it would be the first time Jim would get a glimpse of how her life had evolved since they broke up. She looked around the place, wondering how it would look through his eyes.

She did not adhere to any one type of decorating. Her style was a mishmash of her life. Every piece had a story. The 1950s Formica kitchen set with the turquoise vinyl chairs that had belonged to her grandparents. The cuckoo clock on the living-room wall from her husband's parents—they'd been lovely people —after their trip to Switzerland. The blonde Scandinavian dining-room set she'd picked up at an estate sale. The record player in the corner and the case of LPs she'd collected down through the years before vinyl was retro or cool. On her walls was a mix of contemporary and traditional art. A still-life of fruit over the dining-room cabinet. An abstract work of art in the living room. Whatever caught her fancy or had meaning in her life, she'd bought, never giving a second thought to whether it would match or go with what she already had.

It made her think that she was satisfied with her life. She'd learned after Brad's unexpected death not to take anything for granted. Not to put off to tomorrow what could be done today. And at fifty years of age, she had a happy life: Brent, a nice family, lovely friends, and she was involved in her community.

She'd gone on some amazing trips. Yes, she was content. And she had no intention of disrupting that feeling.

Donna was putting fresh towels and a new bottle of liquid hand soap in the downstairs bathroom when her doorbell rang.

Jim stood in her driveway, holding a platter in his hands.

She turned on the outside light.

"Come on in, Jim," she said. Her stomach felt oddly queasy at the thought of him in her house. Her youthful past encroached on her settled adulthood.

He stepped into her kitchen and set down the platter on her table. A broad grin broke out on his face. "Is this the same table that was in your grandmother's kitchen?"

She nodded and took the platter, which was full of cheese, pepperoni, and olives, and placed it on a shelf in her fridge. It was a little weird that a kitchen table could connect them to the past and to people who were no longer alive.

"It is," she said.

He nodded. "Your grandmother made the best blueberry pie."

"Yes, she did," Donna agreed.

"She didn't leave you the recipe by any chance, did she?" he asked.

Donna nodded. "She did, actually." He seemed to be waiting. Donna hoped he wasn't expecting her to make him one like she used to do when she was a lovestruck teenager. That was never going to happen.

Jim raised one eyebrow, and one corner of his mouth lifted slightly. A silence fell that felt heavy around them. Donna turned her attention to the coffee pot and filled the reservoir with water.

"Have they been gone long?" he asked, hands in his pockets, looking in her direction.

She stopped and turned to look at him. "Gosh, yes. Right after I had Brent. Gramps had a major stroke and Gram insisted on taking care of him, No one could talk her out of it—"

He laughed, bent his head and shook it. "You were so much like her."

She tilted her head and asked with a tight smile, "Are you saying I was stubborn?"

He lifted his head and his bright blue eyes twinkled. "Not at all. Determined is a better word."

"Oh, right," she said softly, pulling a coffee filter from the box. "Anyway, Gram took care of Gramps and unbeknownst to anyone at the time, she had a lump growing in her breast and did nothing about it. Six months after he came home, he had another massive stroke and died in his bed. Gram followed three weeks later. It was awful."

"I'm sorry."

She nodded. Despite their deaths, the memories of her grand-parents made her happy. She couldn't wait to be a grandmother. A great example had been given to her. Now, if only Brent could find a nice girl to settle down with and have some children.

As she scooped coffee into the filter, she asked, "What about your parents?" After Jim had left, his parents had followed him as he was their only child. And after that, Donna had lost touch with them.

He nodded and said solemnly, "They're gone. Mom passed about twenty years ago and Dad just went five years ago. Your parents?"

"Gone as well," she said. She sighed. "Hard to believe they're no longer around to act as a buffer between us and mortality."

Jim snorted. "Tell me about it. We're the buffer now. And it's as unexciting as it gets."

Not wanting to delve into a deep subject, Donna changed the subject. "Are you already bored with retirement?" The Jim she'd known in high school had had a short attention span. He always had to be doing something.

Before he could answer, the doorbell chimed.

"Excuse me," she said, relieved at the arrival of a third party. She could see the top of Sarge's permed head and Ralph's square glasses through the side-door window. She ran down the steps to let them in.

As they followed her into the kitchen, Sarge grumbled about Donna's icy driveway but pulled up short when she spotted Jim standing there in the kitchen.

"Well, Jim, this is a surprise," Sarge said, unsmiling.

"I bet it is," Jim said with a good-natured laugh.

Before Sarge could reply with a sharp retort, Donna asked for help transferring snacks to the dining room.

Under Donna's direction, they carried dishes to the sideboard in the dining room. Sarge took a look at the snacks laid out and sniffed, "Same old, same old." She must have just done her home perm, because there was a strong smell of ammonia around her and her gray curls were tighter than usual. Ralph said quick hellos to everyone and was first in line to get a plate and start piling it up with food.

"Do you always have to be first, Ralph?" Sarge said. "Can you at least wait until everyone gets here?"

Ralph looked sheepish and said, "Sorry, Donna, I worked late tonight and I haven't had any dinner."

"Will I make you a sandwich, Ralph?" Donna asked.

Ralph opened his mouth to answer Donna when Sarge boomed, "No!"

He lowered his head and said, "Maybe not, then."

Donna glanced at Sarge and then thought better of contradicting her. As she walked past Ralph, she whispered, "Just fill up your plate with snacks, Ralph."

"Will do, Donna," he said and gave her a quick salute and a smile.

They had just sat down and Donna was beginning to take notes on a legal pad when she heard the side door open and Christine appeared. They'd been friends long enough that they just walked into each other's houses without knocking. Donna felt everyone should have a friend like that.

Christine was coming from her work as a real-estate agent. She pulled off her coat and laid it on the arm of the sofa. She wore business casual. She held up a platter.

"I've brought seaweed pesto and crackers," she said. "Where will I put them?"

Donna nodded toward the sideboard.

"Seaweed?" Sarge grimaced. "Are you for real, Christine? Who would want to eat anything that people have been wading through with their dirty feet? And you want me to just toss it on a cracker? I don't think so."

"Hey, Sarge, you don't have to eat it," Christine said loudly, and she set the platter down with a thud in the middle of the table. "More for the rest of us." There had been antagonism between the two since 1987 when Christine had been hired as a cashier at the grocery store and Sarge had been the one to train her. There were rumors about a tussle between the two of them in aisle four next to the flour and cake mixes but to this day, Christine would neither confirm nor deny. And no one dared asked Sarge.

"I'll give it a try," Jim said with a little too much enthusiasm. He was rewarded for his efforts with a scowl from Sarge.

"I'll try some, too," Ralph said. But Sarge gave him a little kick beneath the table and Ralph emitted a soft "oomph." He added quickly, "On second thought, I'll pass, Christine."

Frustrated, Donna said, "Does everyone have something to eat? Can we get started?"

Hurriedly, the group filled their plates with snacks and their glasses with beverages.

"We need to talk about some decorations for the festival and what we would like to do indoors and stuff," Donna began.

"I think we should look into ice sculptures," Christine said.

"Ice sculptures?" Sarge frowned. "Because it isn't cold enough?" Every year, Sarge complained about how cold it was going to be for the Snowball Festival. Then when they got together in June to plan the Orchard Falls Independence Day Festival, she complained about how hot it was going to be.

But Donna had to agree with Christine. "I think ice sculptures would be nice." She scribbled on her list. "Do we know anyone who does them?"

Christine smiled. "I'm way ahead of you, Donna. I've made a list. I'll make some calls in the morning."

"That's great. Let's move on. I'm assembling a team of the town's knitters and we're going to yarn bomb Main Street," Donna said.

"Yarn bomb?" Jim asked with confusion.

"Yeah, they're knitting scarves for all the tree trunks lining Main Street," Sarge said sourly.

"It's a little more involved than that," Donna said. All eyes were on her. "It's a type of non-permanent graffiti. I've already spoken to the town's top knitters and they're enthused about it."

"Wielding their needles and ready to go," Jim joked.

Donna stared at him.

"Sorry," he said and coughed.

"Anyway, our plan is to not only decorate the tree trunks lining Main Street but everything else as well, mostly in front of the community center and of course, Horace himself," she said, referring to the statue of the town's founder in the center of town. "The old milk dispenser is going to be done up as well."

She hoped her enthusiasm would be contagious, but the group gave her a blank stare.

"Does anyone here knit?" she asked, looking around the group.

Christine laughed. "Donna, you know I'm not crafty. But if you need anything made from popsicle sticks, I'm your girl."

Christine had led numerous Boy Scout troops for years when her boys were young.

Sarge spoke up. "I tried crocheting once. Everyone said I would find it relaxing. My stitches were so tight, I couldn't get past the sixth row on anything."

Ralph nodded, adding, "We've got lots of unfinished blankets in the house."

Donna moved the meeting on. She didn't want them there all night. After all, she had to get up and go to work in the morning.

It was decided that Jim and Ralph would be responsible for the Christmas tree inside the community center, as well as hanging all the lighting. Donna wondered if Jim had taken on too much. After all, he'd been gone for so long, and it seemed a lot to manage.

As everyone pulled on their winter coats and gloves, Jim seemed to linger and did not reach for his coat right away. Donna wondered if he was going to hang on after the others left. There was no need to. Yet he didn't seem to be leaving. Her heart began to thump.

Once the rest of them were out the side door, Donna began removing things from the dining room and carrying them back to the kitchen.

"Here, let me help you," Jim said as they both reached for his cheese tray.

"I don't need your help," she said. They held onto the tray, neither letting go.

"I know you don't," he said, "but I'd like to."

Sighing, she let go of the tray and picked up a plate of brownies, which Ralph had made a serious dent in. Jim was behind her and it made her nervous. Why did he insist on hanging around? Did he really think they could just pick up where they left off?

Without conversation, they brought everything to the kitchen and laid it on Donna's kitchen table.

"Will you take some of this home?" she asked. "I'll never eat it all."

"Sure, if you don't mind," he said.

She shook her head. "I'd only end up throwing it all out." She took out a Tupperware container and gave him most of the leftovers.

"Listen, Donna, I was wondering if you'd want to go to breakfast tomorrow morning," he asked.

"I'm working," she said. She set the empty dishes in the sink and started running the water.

"Dinner tomorrow night?" he asked.

"I've got plans," she replied.

"What about breakfast Saturday morning?" he pressed.

"Saturday mornings I have my knitting club," she said.

"Do you have any time free in your schedule?" he asked.

"Not really. I work full time and I do a lot of things in my down time," she said.

"You don't have a half an hour anywhere?" He laughed and his eyes twinkled, full of merriment and mischief. Just like they used to. Donna's mouth went dry.

She squirted some dish soap under the running faucet and looked at him. "I don't think it's a good idea."

"Why?"

Was he that obtuse? He really didn't seem to get it.

"Jim, that's all in the past between us," she explained. And that's where she wanted to leave it: in the past. She had no desire to resurrect that relationship from all those years ago. No matter how he made her feel all these years later. Especially a relationship that had left her heartbroken.

"So? Can't we be friends?" he asked with a nervous laugh.

"I don't think it works like that." Too much time had elapsed since she'd last seen him. When he made no moves to depart, she said, "Jim, it's getting late."

"Late?" he enquired. "It's not even ten."

"I've got to get ready for bed."

"Look, I just thought it might be nice to get together and catch up. Compare notes, so to speak," he said with a laugh.

Was everything always so easy for him?

She shook her head and said, "No, I don't think so."

He opened the door and a blast of frigid air blew in. He paused and held up the Tupperware container. "I'll get this back to you."

"There's no hurry," she said.

"Goodnight, Donna," he said quietly and closed the door behind him.

Donna locked the door behind him as if it could keep out the past and all the heightened emotions from that time. As she leaned against the door, she let out a long sigh, as if she'd been holding her breath since he'd arrived.

CHAPTER 4

$\mathcal{T}$he snow that fell overnight left the sidewalks covered in slush. Jim gingerly climbed over a snowbank and stepped out into the street, waiting for a plow to pass. He looked both ways and dashed across the street to Mr. Brenneman's Hardware Store, a place that had been in business for over one hundred years. He'd purposely bypassed the big, brand-name hardware store in favor of this one. This was the place where Jim had had his first part-time job.

At the front of the store, snow shovels lined the wall. When he stepped inside, it was like stepping back in time. Memories of working here after school, on weekends, and through the summers as a teenager slammed him. It still had a faint smell of sawdust and fertilizer. It was a small place with an accumulation of a century's worth of stuff. There were high ceilings and the original wide-plank floors. He saw that someone had finally taken advantage of all that unused space near the ceiling; there was now a variety of toboggans, sleds, and coasters hanging at the top of the walls near the ceiling. He wondered if the kids still went to the hill just outside of town to sled like he and his friends used to do.

He stood in the doorway for a moment, taking in the sights and smells of the place.

"Can I help you?" asked a shaky voice.

Jim turned in the direction of the voice and broke into a broad smile when he recognized Mr. Brenneman. The man appeared to have shrunk with age—Jim figured he had to be close to ninety. He still wore his signature bow-tie and cardigan. His hair had thinned to a few strands on top of his head but his eyes were lively and bright.

"Mr. Brenneman, how are you?" Jim said, extending his hand. "It's me, Jim O'Hara."

He was careful with the man's frail hand in his.

Mr. Brenneman smiled. "Jim! How are you? I heard you were back in town."

Jim nodded, setting his hands on his hips. "Yep. Retired after thirty years of active service."

"From one vet to another, thank you for your service," Mr. Brenneman said.

"My pleasure," Jim said proudly. It had been a career he'd loved. It had cost him his personal life but he had no regrets. He stood by his choices.

"What brings you in here?"

"I'm sourcing Christmas lights for the festival and I wanted to see how you were doing," Jim said.

"Listen, I've got catalogues of Christmas lights and decorations and I can sell them to you at cost," Mr. Brenneman said.

Always the businessman, Jim thought. "That's great. Hey, I thought you had retired."

Mr. Brenneman laughed. "I did. When I turned seventy-five, I retired, and Helen and I did a lot of traveling. It was a great retirement. But then after Helen died, I was bored, so I came back to work. Haven't regretted it since."

"Good. Good for you." Jim couldn't see himself returning to

active military service, though he had yet to figure out where his place was in the world.

"Can I interest you in a bottle of cream soda?" Mr. Brenneman asked. "Come on back and we'll look through the catalogues for some Christmas lights."

"Geez, I haven't had a cream soda in about three decades." Jim laughed.

"Then you're overdue," Mr. Brenneman said with a smile.

JIM WAS THINKING of the pleasant afternoon he'd just spent with his former boss. They'd sat in the back room around Mr. Brenneman's desk, drinking cream soda from glass bottles. It was like the old days. When he left, Jim had felt content. But he couldn't hang around in the back room of the hardware store drinking cream soda for the rest of his life.

When he pulled into his driveway, he saw Donna using a snowblower to clear hers. Since he'd left earlier, about three more inches of snow had fallen. He sat there for a moment, puzzled by her. Was she going to continue to pretend that they hadn't meant anything to each other all those years ago? More than anything, he wanted to get to the bottom of why she hadn't answered the last letter he'd sent before the start of the first Gulf War. That letter had changed his destiny, but not in the way he'd thought it would. And why all the anger that seemed to emanate off of her after all this time? If anyone had the right to be angry, it was him.

Once he parked his SUV, he trotted over to Donna's driveway. Snow crunched beneath his feet and his breath came out in wisps. Her property was covered in Christmas lights. The house, the garage, the front porch, and the lamppost were twinkling in bright colors. He'd seen a young man on a ladder earlier hanging all the exterior lighting. Jim wondered if the man was her son. He looked about Leah's age.

Donna stopped her snowblower when she saw him and leaned against it.

"Hi, Jim," she said. Snow fell around them.

"Look, Donna, I'd like to take you to dinner," Jim started. If she said no, he'd leave her be. He wasn't one to beg, and even he could only take rejection so many times. He wasn't impervious.

Donna sighed. Jim stiffened. Were her memories of their time together that different from his? They'd gone out for almost five years.

"Why does me asking you out for a meal offend you so much?" he asked, beginning to feel aggrieved himself.

"Because you want to go back and revisit the past, and I don't," she said.

He tried a grin. "Some of the past was pretty good, as I recall." He lowered his voice, even though there was no one around. "Remember going up to the park with a blanket and a bottle of peach schnapps?"

Her eyes widened in surprise at the memory but then her features shut down. "Jim, I am really not interested. And I wish you'd stop asking me out—it makes me uncomfortable."

Jim stood there for a moment. This was not the Donna he'd left behind. What had happened in her life that had changed her? Or maybe nothing had. She looked away.

"Okay, then, I won't bother you anymore," he said.

"Thank you," she said firmly. She went to turn the snow-blower back on but he put his hand over hers.

"Wait a minute, Donna," he said.

"Now what?" she asked, her mouth set in a grim line.

"You're angry with me. That's what all this is about. You're mad at me."

"Huh, don't flatter yourself," Donna replied, her face reddening. She turned away from him, turned the snowblower back on, and pushed it hard.

"You're angry!" Jim repeated, raising his voice to be heard above the noise of the snowblower.

"I am not," she yelled, but there was flash of irritation in her eyes.

He reached over and shut the machine down.

She bristled and stood up straight. "I am not angry with you," she said through gritted teeth.

"Who are you trying to convince?" he asked. "Me or you?"

Furious, Donna flipped the snowblower back on. Jim moved to shut it off.

"Talk to me, Donna," Jim said.

"I'd rather not," she said tightly.

"Come on. I really don't understand. Seriously," he said. "If anyone has the right to be angry, it's me."

"You? You have a right to be angry?" Her eyes grew large and her voice rose an octave. "The last time I saw you was when you dumped me! At Christmas! Don't remember? Because I sure do."

"I was getting ready to go off to war. Remember that little thing? I was kind of worried about that!" he shouted.

"Is that a prerequisite for going into battle? Dumping your girlfriend?" she asked, her voice shaking.

"As soon as I got back to base, I realized what a big mistake I'd made," Jim said. "I told you that."

Donna's expression was severe. "When exactly did you tell me this?"

"When I asked you to marry me!" Jim yelled.

The air around them went dead and the silence was burdensome.

Donna spoke first. "I think I would remember if you'd asked me to marry you."

Jim's stance went rigid and he looked dazed. "What are you

talking about? I asked you to marry me and what did I get? Nothing! You couldn't even give me a reply!"

Donna's mouth fell open as she caught a breath. "When did you propose to me? Was I there? Are you sure you're not mixing me up with someone else?"

"Of course not!" he replied angrily. He put his hands on his hips and stared at the ground, at the clean path the snowblower had just made. His thoughts flew back to January 1991. His detachment was already on the ground in the Mideast for the war that was definitely coming.

He huffed impatiently and looked at her. "I sent you a letter. I wrote it on January 16th, 1991, the night before we went to war. In that letter, I asked you to marry me."

Donna folded her arms across her chest. "You did not."

"I know what the hell I wrote, Donna," he said. "Look, I knew we were going to war, and the only thing I wanted was for you to know my intentions: that I wanted to spend the rest of my life with you!"

Donna wobbled and leaned against the snowblower. In a voice he could barely hear, she said, "I never got that letter."

Jim frowned. "What do you mean?"

She looked at him. "Just what I said. I never got any letter from you after we broke up, and definitely not one with a marriage proposal."

"You're not serious," he said, the ramifications of that missing letter beginning to swirl around them and settle like snow.

"I am," she said. "Come in, I'll show you."

Donna left the snowblower right there in the middle of her driveway and went in through the side door of her house. Jim followed her inside. In the small hallway, Donna stepped onto the first step, turned around, and rubbed the heel of her boot against the edge of the step. Jim was transported back in time and it unnerved him. Donna used to do that with all her boots. He could almost hear Mrs. Van Dyke's voice from the past, chiding her daughter about ruining a perfectly good pair of boots. Maybe this wasn't such a good idea. Too many memories, he thought. The weight of them was more than he could bear.

Donna removed her coat and indicated he should do the same. She took the coats and hung them on hooks in the back hall.

"Sit down," she said, nodding toward the kitchen table. "I'll be right back." Donna disappeared and he heard her going up the stairs.

Jim pulled out a chair and sat down. He looked around. There was an aroma of orange, cinnamon, and cloves.

Donna returned with a rectangular floral box in her hands. She set it down in the middle of the table. She opened a cabinet door and asked, "I have eggnog or mulled wine. Which would you prefer?"

"Mulled wine," he said.

Donna set two wine glasses on the counter and poured mulled wine from a pot on the stove. As she joined Jim at the table, she handed him a glass.

Neither said anything. They both sipped their wine. Donna lifted the lid off the box and Jim saw a stack of letters, yellowed with age. He recognized the familiar scrawl as his own on the top, military-issued envelope. She'd saved every one of his letters. She'd gone on to marry someone else and yet she'd saved every one of his letters.

He coughed to cover the emotions that welled up within him.

She laid her hands over the top of the box. "I have every letter you sent me, from the time you went away to college to right before you came home that Christmas." After she put on a pair of reading glasses, she removed the first letter from the stack. She took the pages out of the envelope. "This was the first letter I received from you, when you went away to college," she said quietly.

He'd been two years ahead of her in school. It had been difficult leaving her behind. They wrote, and they spoke on the phone when they could, but only briefly because it had been so expensive back then. Not to mention it hadn't been very private. He'd be on the pay phone in the hall of his dorm, and he could hardly say what was on his mind, not with all those guys around. And he tried to make it home once a month to see Donna. They carried on like that until he graduated from college and she'd just entered the local college. In May of 1990, he'd graduated with a degree in history and had enlisted in the army. But then in the summer of 1990, in a place far away from their own little world, Iraq invaded Kuwait, and the consequences would play out personally in their own lives.

He was still trying to process the fact that she had never received his proposal.

Donna pulled the first letter out and began to read aloud.

Jim sat back in his chair and stared at his glass of mulled wine, but didn't really see it. He was thinking of the words he'd written to her all those years ago, lying on his bed in his dorm room, when his whole life was in front of him. A life that was to include Donna by his side.

Donna read each letter out loud. Midway through, she stood up and put together a plate of Christmas cookies. When she set the plate down in front of him, he looked at her and saw that her eyes were wet.

"Did you want another glass of wine?" she asked, her voice suddenly high.

He shook his head. "No thanks."

"Will I make a pot of coffee?" she asked. "We've still got the rest of the box to go through." She paused and then added quickly, "Unless of course, you don't want to."

"No, I want to go through all of them," he said quietly. "Coffee is good."

He was grateful for the change to a topic of something as mundane as coffee. His insides were in a turmoil. This was what repercussions and consequences felt like. For the first time, he could feel it physically. It felt like a kick in the gut.

Nothing was said as Donna moved around the kitchen making coffee. The air around them was charged with what might have been. And all that had been lost. She made them sandwiches and set them on the table with two cups of coffee. Before she sat down, she put sugar and creamer in the middle of the table.

After she fixed her coffee, she put her cheaters back on and picked up the next letter. They sat like that for the next hour, sipping coffee and eating sandwiches. Closing his eyes, he listened to her voice, thinking it sounded pretty much like it had three decades before.

"Jim, have you fallen asleep?"

He opened his eyes and shook his head. "No. When we used to talk on the phone, I always closed my eyes so I could concentrate on just your voice."

"I didn't know that," Donna said.

He gave her small smile. "Now you do."

She'd arrived at the last letter. She read it slowly, her voice breaking on the last line: "All my love forever, Jim." Quickly, she pulled herself together. But Jim noticed her chin quivering. Without looking at him, she folded the letter and slid it carefully back into its envelope.

"That was the last letter I had from you," she said quietly. "It was dated December 8th."

Neither said anything. They sat there with the box of letters from decades ago between them.

Jim finally spoke. "I wanted you to marry me, Donna."

Donna nodded.

"Do you believe me?" he asked.

She looked down at her hands in her lap and nodded her head. "Yes," she said softly.

"But you never got the letter," he stated. For the first time in his life, he felt old. And weary.

"When you were home at Christmas, you just weren't yourself," Donna said. "You were so anxious."

"I knew that the probability of me going into war was very high. I was nervous."

Donna regarded him with a thoughtful expression.

"I didn't know how long the war was going to last and I didn't want you tied down, waiting around for me."

"I would have waited." She sighed.

"Do you remember our very last conversation? The last thing you said to me?" he asked.

"I do." She looked down at her hands, folded on the table. "I said you could change your mind about ending things between us, and to just let me know." For a minute, Donna didn't say anything, as if she was trying to gather her thoughts. "I knew you were stressed and I wanted you to know that you could take it back."

"That's all I thought of when I went back. I kept asking myself, 'What did you just do, you idiot?'"

"When I never heard back, I just assumed you were serious about breaking up."

"Oh, Donna," he groaned.

The reality of the situation bogged them down.

Jim finally stood up, his legs feeling heavy, as if he'd been walking through sand on a hot day. "I should go."

"Okay." Donna nodded without looking at him. She went out to the back hall and grabbed his jacket.

"I'll see you around," he said quietly. He needed to get out of there. The thought of going home depressed him. More than anything, he needed to walk. The cold, crisp night air would clear his head.

"Do you still have my letters?" Donna asked.

With great regret, Jim shook his head. "No, I don't. I'm sorry. After Carol and I were married, she found them and threw them out."

"Oh, okay," Donna said.

Was it? Jim wondered, as he pulled on his coat and headed down the stairs.

"Your husband didn't mind you'd saved those letters?" he asked.

Donna shook her head. "No."

Jim paused with his hand on the door. He turned and looked up at her. Her arms were crossed. She wore a heavy navy sweater and a pair of jeans. And she was still as beautiful as he remembered.

"Donna, can I ask you a question?"

She nodded. He drank her in: the auburn hair, the bright green eyes. He had to know. It would be some sort of closure at least, no matter what the answer.

"If that letter hadn't been lost, if you'd seen my proposal . . ." he said, swallowing hard. He did not take his eyes off her. "What would your answer have been?"

Donna did not hesitate. "Yes. My answer would have been yes."

CHAPTER 5

*W*here it had seemed Jim was popping up everywhere, just as suddenly, he'd disappeared. Days went by without Donna seeing him again. At work, she glanced out the window regularly, hoping to get a glimpse of him somewhere on Main Street.

The revelation of that lost letter had left Donna reeling. Without a doubt, she knew that if she had received that letter, she would have married Jim. And although she'd always wanted to remain in Orchard Falls, at twenty, she would have gone anywhere with him. The knowledge that had she received that letter her life would have gone on a much different trajectory occupied every waking thought. At first. But then, one evening in her kitchen as she waited for Brent to stop over after work, she started thinking about her late husband, Brad.

Brad had been in her business class at college. She'd hardly noticed him because he was so quiet and always sat in the back of the classroom. Brad had been the complete opposite of Jim. Three months after Jim had dumped her, Brad had approached her one day after class and asked her out, and she'd said yes, her only goal being to forget Jim and recover from her heartbreak. A rebound relationship.

But then a funny thing had happened. As she got to know Brad, she'd realized he had a thoughtful manner, he was kind, and he was funny. They shared the same values, and their opposite personalities acted as a magnet. Within eighteen months, they had married and Brent had come along. Their marriage, though cut short, had been a happy one.

"Hi, Mom," called a voice from the hallway.

"I'm in here," Donna replied.

Her kitchen table was covered in baking trays of dog treats in the shapes of stars, bells, and candy canes. A half-empty jar of peanut butter and a pile of carrot peels littered her countertop.

Brent appeared and her eyes filled with tears at the sight of her only child. How on earth could she ever regret not marrying Jim? If she had married Jim, there would have been no Brad. There would be no Brent. Her shoulders sagged as relief flooded through her. Everything was going to be all right. Everything had worked out the way it was supposed to.

"I see you've been busy," Brent said with a laugh.

"Just making some treats for your patients at the clinic," Donna said with a smile.

"Mom, you're the best!" Brent said.

Donna turned around and gave a little sniff, not wanting Brent to see her eyes welling up. She soaked the measuring cups and spoons in the mixing bowl in the sink. Cleanup could wait until later.

"I'm sorry I'm late," Brent said. "Mrs. Jackson's collie had a reaction to a new dog food so I waited for her to bring the dog into the clinic."

Pride filled Donna. He'd probably stayed late to help that dog instead of referring them to the emergency vet hospital. When it came to animals, he couldn't say no. Knowing that she'd raised a good man was very satisfying.

"I'm glad to hear it. Mrs. Jackson would be heartbroken if anything happened to that dog," Donna said. "Sit down, Brent, I've saved you some dinner."

Brent washed his hands and pulled up a chair at the table. Donna popped a bowl of homemade beef stew into the microwave. She poured her son a tall glass of water and set it in front of him. When the microwave beeped, she pulled the bowl out and gave it a quick stir with a spoon before setting it in front of him.

"I ran into Mary Ellen Schumacher today," Brent said.

"Really?"

Brent reddened. "Six-month checkup. She is my dentist, after all."

Donna waited. There would be more to this. Brent wouldn't just mention something so casually.

Once he finished chewing, he said, "She wants me to run the talent show for the Festival! Can you imagine me running a talent show?" He paused. "Boy, she doesn't take no for an answer. It was hard to refuse her; I felt captive in the chair." He laughed.

Donna didn't approve when Brent disparaged himself. "Well, why not?"

He grinned and looked at her. "I have no talent, remember? Violin lessons? Soccer? Karate?" He bent his head, shaking it, and laughed. "I was hopeless!"

"You weren't hopeless!" Donna protested. She wished he wouldn't talk about himself like that.

Brent's fork and knife paused midair and he looked at his mother, raising an eyebrow. "Mom, come on."

"Well, maybe you weren't talented in those things, but look how talented you are with animals," she started.

"Mom!" he protested with a laugh.

"No, Brent, seriously. Who took care of that baby bird who fell out of the nest? What about that other bird with the broken wing? And who stopped at the side of the road to take that cat who'd been run over to the vet?"

Brent shrugged. "I didn't do anything anyone else wouldn't have done."

"And don't forget Howard," she continued, referring to his childhood pet. No dog was able to do more tricks than Howard.

"Yeah, Howie was a great dog," Brent said fondly. "He was so intelligent."

"Nonsense." Donna shook her head. "You're a healer. And that is a talent the world could definitely use more of," she said with conviction.

Brent laughed and said good-naturedly, "What, like an animal whisperer?"

"Exactly like that!" Donna said. She could see he didn't believe her. "Do you know how many birds I tried to help as a kid?"

He shook his head and took a gulp of water. When he realized her question wasn't a rhetorical one, he asked, "How many?"

"Four in total," she responded. "And they all died. Not one made it."

He gave half a shrug.

"Mary Ellen asked you to be in charge of the talent show, that's all. It's not like she asked you to dance and sing. It would be nice for you to get involved with the festival in some aspect," she said.

"I am involved," Brent protested.

Donna tilted her head and gave him a smirk. "Printing up and handing out pamphlets about how pets aren't just for Christmas morning hardly constitutes being involved."

"I think it does," he said.

"Just think about it. Running the talent show, that is," she said to encourage him. "I mean really, how hard could it be?"

Brent stared at her. "Pretty hard!"

By the time Brent had finished his bowl of candy cane ice cream, Donna had convinced him that running the talent show was just the thing for him to get involved with the community. This would be good for Brent, Donna concluded. It would get him out there. More involved. And most of all, mingling with other people.

ON SATURDAY MORNING, Donna left her house a few minutes earlier than usual to walk up to the library on Main Street for the weekly knitting meeting. She had her canvas bag of knitting supplies on her arm. She looked over at Jim's house but all was quiet. His car was not in the driveway. It had now been almost a week since he'd left her house. She hoped he was doing okay. Their discovery had been a blow but there was nothing that could be done about it now. No sense lingering in the past. It was over and behind them.

She made her way through the slush, head down so she could keep an eye on the sidewalk. A car passed her and gave a beep of the horn. When she looked up, she saw Jim going by. She waved as his car disappeared down the street.

The ladies were already gathered at the library in one of the meeting rooms. On a long table against the wall, everyone had laid out what they had completed for the yarn bombing. Most of the members were milling around the table, admiring each other's work and fretting about whether there was enough time to get everything done.

Betty Held called the meeting together. It was a loose group with no real structure but it worked; they'd been gathering at the library for the last five years and knitting to their hearts' content. Betty was a natural-born leader and everyone else in the group was quite happy to let her run things informally. For thirty years, Betty had cared for foster children. The general consensus was that if she could do that, she could certainly corral a bunch of knitters.

Once the group quieted down, Betty said, "I've got some bad news."

The group hushed and waited. Donna hoped no one had died. Death was hard enough, but around the holidays it was so much worse.

"Mary Ellen Schumacher broke her wrist yesterday," Betty announced.

Everybody gasped. The woman next to Donna threw her hand to her chest as if she were trying to hold herself together physically. Someone asked, "Is she all right?"

"She is. She'll be coming home from the hospital today." Betty paused. "Mary Ellen called me last night. She's going to ask all the heads of the committees to take on some extra responsibilities."

Donna made a mental note to stop over and see Mary Ellen later.

Moving on to the next order of business, Betty went over what they had and what they still needed. Like a commander rallying her troops, she encouraged everyone to step up their game.

The only one sitting was Alice Kempf, Orchard Falls's oldest resident at ninety-eight. Her cat, Mavis, was the oldest in town at twenty-two. In her gnarled hands was a pair of knitting needles that flew automatically. Alice, a former schoolteacher who'd never married, had been knitting for as long as anyone in town could remember. Donna was pretty sure every baby ever born in Orchard Falls had a knitted cap gifted by Alice in their possession. She'd been placed in charge of knitting a scarf for the statue of Horace, the town's founder. Alice's scarf for Horace was blue with intricate white snowflakes. It was gorgeous.

Donna nodded toward Alice and said, "That's beautiful, Alice. Old Horace is going to look good in that."

Alice regarded her with her bright blue eyes. "I think so. It's nice that there's someone in town older than me."

Donna laughed. "And you're making his scarf!"

Alice crowed and the knitting needles never stopped moving. Donna sat down in the chair next to Alice. She set her bag down on the floor next to her and pulled out her needles and yarn. She was in the midst of making something for one of the many tree trunks on Main Street. She'd been assigned three trees in front of the bank and the bakery. She'd gotten their measurements and had begun work immediately.

Alice leaned into Donna and asked, "What's this I hear Jim O'Hara is back in town? And living next door to you!"

Donna noticed the older woman, despite her advanced years, did not drop a stitch. Alice's eyes were keen as she waited for Donna to answer.

"Yes, he is," Donna said. She laughed. "Funny, isn't it? How he ended up living next to me?"

Alice nodded. "Must be fate."

Donna raised her eyebrows. "Must be."

"You know, everyone used to think you two would end up married," Alice said. "The two of you seemed so well suited to each other."

Donna shrugged.

"What happened?"

Donna opened her mouth to say what she'd told herself all these years since, that he'd gone off to war and she'd never heard from him again, but that version of the story no longer rang true. She gave Alice a quick smile, more to reassure herself than anyone else. "It was fate that broke us up."

"And maybe it's fate that has brought you back together," Alice suggested.

Donna spoke hurriedly. "Oh, he just moved in next door. We're not dating or anything."

"Not yet," Alice said with a smile.

"Alice Kempf," Donna said, looking at her. "You're the one who once said the reason for your longevity was the fact that you'd never married."

Alice grimaced. "That was in an interview for my 95th birthday. The questions the interviewer asked were mind-numbing." She rolled her eyes. "So, I livened it up a bit to make things interesting."

Donna regarded the other woman with a grin. "You lied?"

Alice cringed. "Lied is a strong word. Embellished is a better one."

Donna laughed. "So you don't drink a beer a day?"

Alice shook her head. "No, of course not." She paused and lowered her voice, "But I do have a shot of whiskey every night before going to bed."

When Donna stopped laughing, she asked. "So you don't credit not marrying for your longevity?"

Alice's smile disappeared and she said soberly, "Oh, I do. But that's not to say I wouldn't have liked to be married. Or at least asked. Just so I could have said no." And then the oldest woman in Orchard Falls got a fit of the giggles, and Donna joined her.

Everyone left in good humor and Donna stopped at the town's coffee shop and got a chai latte to go. She loved the blended smell of cinnamon, cardamom, and nutmeg. She walked down Main Street, looking at all the Christmas displays in the windows. The town's volunteers were stringing lights across the street and several people had been tasked with hanging either giant red ornaments or silvery snowflakes from the lampposts. Speakers had been set up around town and Judy Garland's rendition of "Have

Yourself a Merry Little Christmas" floated out along Main Street as snow fell. It was magical.

Donna loved this time of year in town. Once she reached the end of one side of Main Street, she looked both ways before crossing the street and walked back up the other side. She threw her empty cup into a garbage bin and headed in the direction of home. Donna was halfway up the block when she saw Jim walking in her direction. He trudged along, shoulders hunched, head down, and it reminded her of high-school Jim. He'd always been tall. He was six foot by the time he started high school and by the end of it, he was towering at six four. While they were dating, he'd confided in her how his height made him feel self-conscious. This Jim walking toward her reminded her of that old vulnerability of his.

"Hey, Jim," she said as he neared her.

His head shot up, surprised. "Oh, hi. I didn't see you there."

She gave him a warm smile, "No, you wouldn't when you're looking down at the ground."

He laughed but looked away. "It's good to see you, Donna."

He made to walk on, but she reached out for him, looking at him in confusion.

"Are you all right?" she asked. Concern flooded her.

"Yeah, sure, why?" he said hurriedly.

"Jim," Donna said quietly. It pained her to see him looking so preoccupied. Back in school, she'd thought he was the handsomest man she'd ever seen. Those eyes, the broad cheekbones, and the square jaw. After all this time, she still thought he was the most handsome man she'd ever seen.

"What, Donna?" he said, looking distracted.

"It's just that I haven't seen you around," Donna explained. She lowered her voice because people, all wrapped up against the weather, walked past them. She wished they were anywhere else but the middle of the sidewalk on Main Street.

"I thought that's what you wanted," Jim said sharply.

Donna flinched. "I never said *that*."

"I won't be bothering you anymore," he said.

She laughed nervously. "That seems extreme."

Jim looked up and down the street. "Look, Donna, I've got to get home. Leah is coming in today."

"Is Leah your daughter?" she asked, searching his face.

"Yeah, she is," he said. He looked around as if he either didn't want to be seen with her or was looking for an escape.

"Jim, maybe we could sit down and talk," she suggested softly.

He looked at her. "That's not necessary." He paused, glanced at his watch and said, "I've got to go. See you around." And he trotted off.

Donna remained rooted to the sidewalk, watching him leaving, her mouth slightly open.

"Oh, Jim," she whispered.

DONNA HURRIED HOME, made a pot of cream-of-cauliflower soup, and took it over to Mary Ellen Schumacher's house.

Mary Ellen lived in a big, old, rambling Victorian on the residential section of Main Street. Her dental practice occupied the front of the former living quarters of the downstairs. The back rooms downstairs and the second and third floors had been converted into a living space for the dentist.

Donna parked her car in the empty parking lot and went to the back door. She knocked, stepped inside, and called out, "Mary Ellen?"

"In here," came a voice from the other room.

Donna wiped her boots on the mat and stepped into Mary

Ellen's kitchen. After she set the pot on the stove, she followed the sound of the voice into the living room.

Mary Ellen sat in a recliner with her feet up. Her right arm was set in a cast and rested on a pillow. Next to her chair was her orange canary, Creamsicle, in a big cage. With Donna's arrival, he hopped around his cage, chirping, his wings flapping, but soon settled down. There was a giant Christmas tree in the corner of the room that took up a lot of space but filled the air with a beautiful pine scent.

"Oh, Mary Ellen, what happened?" Donna asked at the sight of her.

Mary Ellen muted the television and set her book down, using an envelope as a bookmark.

"Sit down, Donna," she instructed.

Donna sat down on the sofa across the room from Mary Ellen and removed her coat.

"One minute I was walking across the parking lot, the next minute I was putting out my arms and breaking my fall. It happened so fast, I don't know what happened," she said.

Donna winced in sympathy. "Maybe black ice?"

"Probably." Mary Ellen sighed. "Of course, it had to be my right hand—it couldn't have been my left."

"That's too bad. Is there anything I can do?" Donna asked.

"Actually, there is. I was going to call you tonight and see if you would mind taking over my role in running the festival," Mary Ellen said.

Donna's eyes widened and her mouth fell open. "Me?" she asked in disbelief.

"Why not you?" Mary Ellen asked.

"Because I don't have any experience," Donna said. She shifted uncomfortably on the sofa, trying to figure a way to refuse without hurting the other woman's feelings.

"I had no experience either when I started," Mary Ellen said.

"You've been involved in the Snowball Festival for as long as I have."

"And I've always been happy with a subordinate role."

"Yes, but now it's time to move up," Mary Ellen pushed.

"Surely there are people more qualified to take over than me," Donna pointed out. At the same time, she racked her brain trying to think of someone. Christine came to mind but she wouldn't be too happy if Donna volunteered her without her knowledge or consent. Sarge flashed through her thoughts but Donna wouldn't do that to the people of Orchard Falls. She still had to live there when this thing was over.

"I can't think of one," Mary Ellen said.

Donna hesitated.

"I'll only be a phone call away. Besides, once the committees are set up—and they are—they more or less are run by their leaders. Your job is to keep everyone on track. Go to one meeting and then keep in touch by email, phone call, or text." She paused and looked Donna straight in the eye. "I wouldn't ask you if I didn't have faith in you."

Donna wanted to sigh and groan but she pasted a smile on her face and said, "Sure, Mary Ellen, no problem. I can take over."

"Thanks, Donna, that takes a load off my mind."

They chatted for another half hour but Donna's newfound role skated at the back of her mind. Before she left, she heated up some soup for Mary Ellen and buttered a bread roll and served it to her. She didn't leave until she'd washed the dishes and put the soup in the fridge and Mary Ellen was set with a cup of hot chocolate.

As she left, she promised to be in touch with Mary Ellen to get the names and numbers of those in charge of the other committees.

She closed the door behind her, wondering what she had just agreed to do. And most of all, was she capable of doing it?

CHAPTER 6

*J*im spotted Leah's car in his driveway as he approached the house and he picked up his pace, pushing all thoughts of Donna out of his mind. He was breathless and shivering from the cold as he unlocked his side door, and welcomed the heat that greeted him as he opened it.

"Leah!" he called out, bounding into his kitchen. As he did, her cat Tiny waltzed by. That caused Jim to smile. He was even glad to see the cat. "I see you've already made yourself at home," he said to the little feline.

Leah ran down the stairs. He wanted to cry at the sight of her. Right now, she was the only thing he was sure of in the world.

His daughter had his blue eyes but her mother's blonde, fair-haired looks. "Dad!" she cried, landing in front of him and throwing her arms around him.

He took his only child in his embrace and held her tight. When they pulled apart, he had a lot of questions for her. "Were you waiting long? When did you get in? Are you tired?"

Leah laughed. "Dad, come up for air! I got here about half an hour ago but I remembered you'd said there was a spare key under the flowerpot outside." Her smile disappeared and she asked, "That was okay, wasn't it?"

"Of course, of course!" he said. "This is your home, too, honey. And I wouldn't want you sitting out in the cold." He pulled open a catch-all drawer and removed a spare key. "Here, I had a key made for you."

Leah pocketed it. "Thanks. And I'm not tired. Actually, I'm hungry," she said.

"Good, there's a new vegan restaurant that opened, and I thought we could go there," he said. While she was home visiting, he'd respect her commitment and refrain from eating his usual carnivorous fare.

"That sounds great," she said. "Let me just finish unpacking and I'll be ready."

"Good, take your time." He nodded quickly. "How's your mother?"

"She's fine." Leah peered at him. "Are you all right? You seem tense. Nervous."

"I'm fine," he said with a wave of his hand.

As Leah walked through his living room, she glanced around and said, "I see it's minimalism again this year with the Christmas decorations." As she ran up the staircase, Jim could hear her laughing.

He was so glad she was there.

LEAH'S PRESENCE added a welcome distraction to the sobering reality of that one lost letter and how it had irrevocably changed Jim's life in ways he had not imagined back in high school.

Jim knew he couldn't ignore Donna forever, especially since she lived next door. On reflection, he admitted to himself that Donna had always been the love of his life. He'd known it in high school, he knew it in college and he never knew it more clearly than when he penned that letter right before the start of Desert Storm. He'd thought of her often over the ensuing years with nostalgia for what had been lost. His fifty-three-year-old self wished he could go back and kick his twenty-five-year-old self in the back end. Why hadn't he written her or called when he didn't receive a reply from her? Why? He knew the reason. Because his male pride had been wounded. He'd thrown himself into his career. And then one night, a year after his return from Iraq, he'd met a girl named Carol. She was pretty. And then she ended up pregnant. And he'd done what he thought was the right thing and married her. Which turned out to be disastrous. The only good thing to come out of that was Leah.

He mulled over these things as he made coffee at five in the morning. It was still pitch- black outside. A quick glance out the window showed Donna's house shrouded in darkness. He was glad someone was able to sleep.

Hazel, Leah's black-and-gray-striped cat, wound her way around Jim's legs, meowing.

Jim looked down at her. "Why are you up so early?" Jim had never had pets, as he was always moving around or going abroad during his career. But he did like Hazel. She was a nice cat.

There was a clank and then the sound of forced heat from the vent as the furnace stirred to life. Hazel continued to meow and rub up against Jim's legs as he fixed himself a cup of coffee.

Before he took his first sip, he picked up the cat and held her. "Would you like your breakfast now?"

The cat purred loudly, and Jim took this as a yes and set her down on the floor. In the pantry, he found the cans of cat food Leah had picked up at the grocery store stacked on the shelf. After scanning them, he looked down at Hazel, who was looking up at him. "Chicken or fish?" Hazel responded with a meow. "I see Leah hasn't forced her vegan lifestyle on you."

He chose the fish-flavored one, thinking briefly that if the cat was allowed to eat chicken and fish, maybe he could sneak a steak or two by Leah without too much protest. With the sound of the can opener, the other cat, Tiny, made an appearance in the doorway. Jim rolled his eyes. You couldn't use a can opener in this house without an audience with expectations.

"I suppose you want breakfast, too," Jim said. He filled both dishes and the cats parked themselves in front of them. He picked up his coffee mug, sat down at the kitchen table, and was soon lost in the past.

January 1991

In his tent, in the middle of the desert, Jim realized he'd made a big mistake. What had he been thinking? What had possessed him to break up with Donna? Of all the stupid things to do! If only he could put everything on hold—hop on a plane and go back to Orchard Falls and apologize.

The air on the base crackled with excitement, uncertainty, and confusion. He wiped sweat off his brow for the one hundredth time. He made a vow that if he made it home alive, he'd never again complain about how cold winter was. If he made it home . . .

He couldn't get the image of Donna out of his mind. She'd looked absolutely devastated. He'd never felt worse in his life, but at the time he felt he was doing the right thing. Now, he worried that he might not make it home to tell her he'd made a mistake. Or worse, that she'd meet someone else in the meantime. He groaned, ignoring the fact that war was looming large over him at the moment.

He needed her to know how he really felt about her. Hurriedly, he grabbed a sheet of paper and his pen and began to write:

Dear Donna,

When I left you at Christmas, you said if I ever changed my mind about us breaking up to let you know.
This is me, letting you know. This is me changing my mind.
I've made a terrible mistake. A huge mistake in breaking up with you. Please forgive me.
When I was home and there was all this talk of war, I thought nothing would frighten me more than going into battle. But I was wrong. The thing that frightens me most is going ahead in life without you by my side. I can do anything—including survive a war—as long as I know you'll be there for me.
There is no one I could ever love more than you. No one.
I want to spend the rest of my life with you. I want us to be together, side by side in this crazy adventure called life.
I love you, Donna, and I'm asking you to marry me.
I ruined your Christmas, but I promise to make it up to you, next Christmas and every Christmas after.
All my love forever,
Jim

JIM DIDN'T KNOW what to do with himself. For now there was Leah and the preparations for the Snowball Festival to occupy his time, but what would he do in the bleak, cold month of January when Christmas was over? The idea of Florida flitted across his mind and he supposed he could head south for the rest of the winter months. He had buddies all over Florida he could visit. But the thought of heading south by himself depressed him.

The familiar *thunk* of the morning paper landing on the front porch stirred him from his reveries. He pulled his bathrobe tighter around him and padded to the front door in his slippers. Before he opened the front door, he slipped on his boots and stepped outside into a mound of snow that had drifted onto his porch. Shivering, he grabbed the plastic-wrapped paper and brought it inside, shutting the door quietly behind him so as not to wake his daughter upstairs. He kicked off his boots and slipped back into his slippers, heading to the kitchen for another cup of coffee. Jim unfurled the paper and laid it out on the table. He'd just scanned the headlines when he noticed the lights going on in Donna's house next door. He stared for a moment, his thoughts beginning to drift. He gave his head a good shake and turned his focus back to the paper.

JIM WANDERED into the hardware store to check on the status of the lights for the festival. His old boss was busy with a customer at the service counter but he waved at Jim in acknowledgement. Jim nodded in return and set about walking the aisles and examining the contents of the shelves in the small store. After about ten minutes, Mr. Brenneman met him in the aisle. Jim had just grabbed a gallon of windshield-washer fluid off the shelf.

"That's on sale this week," Mr. Brenneman said.

"Good," Jim said.

"How are you, Jim?"

"Good," he said. "Just thought I'd stop by and see if the lights were in yet."

"Actually, I got a batch of lights the other day, but they were too small and I sent them back."

"Do you know when the new sets will be in?" Jim asked.

"They assure me they'll be here within the week," Mr. Brenneman replied.

That would be plenty of time before the festival. Jim nodded. "That's great."

"Can I interest you in a bottle of cream soda?" Mr. Brenneman asked with a grin.

Jim laughed. "I'm going to have to take a rain check."

"All right."

"I'll see you around, Mr. Brenneman," Jim said.

"Are you all right, Jim? You seem a bit out of sorts," Mr. Brenneman said, his usually relaxed face frowning in concern.

Jim shrugged. He didn't want to get into the revelation of his lost letter to Donna. For now, and maybe forever, he wanted to keep that private. "Just trying to find my way."

"Retirement can be tricky. You're still young, and I bet most of your friends are still in the work force," Mr. Brenneman noted. "Except for me. You're stuck with me."

Jim let out a bark of laughter, feeling some of the stress depart his body. But he thought of Donna, Steve, and his friends in the military who still worked.

"May I offer some unsolicited advice?"

"Yes," Jim said.

"You've got too much time on your hands. It can be difficult to transition from a forty- to fifty-hour work week to all the free time in the world. But there are a couple of cures for that. First, you could go back to work," he said. When Jim grimaced in response, Mr. Brenneman added, "Okay, then develop some hobbies. What about genealogy?"

Jim scowled. "Running around cemeteries looking for dead relatives? I'm not too keen on some of my living ones."

Mr. Brenneman laughed. "You're a hoot. How about doing some volunteer work? All this time on your hands will only lead you to thinking about yourself. And that can sometimes lead to trouble. Now don't get me wrong. A little bit of introspection is a good thing. But too much of any good thing is a bad thing. Think about other people instead. Help them out. You'd make a marvelous mentor."

"Oh, I don't know about that," Jim said, looking away and shuffling his feet.

"There are lots of places right here in town that are screaming for volunteers, especially around Christmas time." He paused and added thoughtfully, "Not everyone finds Christmas a happy time of year."

Jim thought back to his first Christmas after his divorce, when he didn't see Leah over the holiday season, and how awful that had been. "Unfortunately, I do know about that firsthand."

The bell over the door tinkled, indicating a customer. They both glanced toward the door. Jim stuck out his hand and Mr. Brenneman shook it.

"Thanks, Mr. Brenneman, I'll let you get back to work."

"Think about what I said. Get involved with things that interest you. Put others first and you'll settle in to your retire-ment," the older man said with a warm smile.

"I will keep that in mind," Jim replied. He said goodbye and headed out the door, taking his advice under consideration.

Outside, he hunched his shoulders and braced himself against the bitter northwesterly wind that howled as it blew through town. He went over in his mind all the things his former boss had said, looking for the answer.

CHAPTER 7

christmas was Donna's favorite time of year. She and Brent always went to Christmas Eve service at the church on Main Street, and she made a turkey and a ham for Christmas Day dinner just like her own mother had done. Once in a while, her older sister came into town with her family, which Donna loved because it meant a full house, but she wasn't coming this year because her daughter had just had her first baby and they wanted to be close to home. But the Christmas season was also a busy season.

Although Donna loved her job at the bank, after almost thirty years, she was looking forward to retirement. She'd started at the bank right out of college as a teller and had worked her way up to financial advisor. It was on these cold, dark winter mornings that thoughts of retirement filled her head.

An early riser by nature, she wasn't planning on spending her days sleeping in. There was so much she wanted to do. The thought of all the new things she'd be able to do with her free time filled her with excitement. There were hobbies, volunteering, and new adventures waiting for her. And the thought of possible grandchildren made her almost giddy.

Since Mary Ellen had asked her to take over the running of the Snowball Festival, she'd had some time to get used to the idea and had more or less resigned herself to it. Lots of deep breathing was helping. Mary Ellen had given her a list of all activities and events planned for the festival and the phone numbers of those running the committees for such events and activities. The previous night, Donna had had to lay her knitting needles aside in order to meet up with the people overseeing those committees. Although by the time the meeting ended, she'd been assured that all was in hand, she couldn't help but feel personally responsible.

There'd likely be no knitting tonight either, as her own committee was meeting at her house. Switching gears mentally, she focused on what needed to be done before the committee meeting later that night at her house.

Everyone was on time, so the meeting got under way promptly.

As soon as everyone had their snacks and gathered around the dining-room table, Sarge lobbed an opening volley with, "I hear you're taking over from Mary Ellen."

"I am," Donna said.

"It's a big task," Sarge said. "Do you think you're qualified?"

Christine butted in. "Donna is more than able to run this year's festival."

Sarge practically gave Christine the stink eye for interrupting. Before the conversation could escalate between the two women, there was the sound of squealing tires outside and they all turned to the front window.

"That didn't sound good," Ralph observed.

After only a brief pause, Sarge launched into a new line of complaint. "I don't understand why they can't come up with some new Christmas music. I mean, I'm sick of listening to the same old tunes that have been around for decades. Gimme a break!"

They all looked at her. Donna decided not to engage. It was a policy that had served her well in the past in regards to Sarge. Jim remained uncharacteristically quiet through it all.

But Christine couldn't resist a chance to challenge her former coworker. "Aw come on, Sarge, you can't mean that!" she said with a laugh.

Donna shot her best friend a look.

Slowly, Sarge turned her head to Christine and leveled her gaze at her, "Why would you think I would say something I didn't mean? Your statement has me at a loss."

Christine burst out laughing. "Come on, Sarge, lighten up."

Donna glanced nervously at Sarge, whose face had gone beet red. Then she glanced at Christine and wondered if she'd lost her mind. Christine knew better than to wind up Sarge. Maybe she'd had too much wine to drink. Donna was just about to intervene when there was the sound of banging on her side door. Donna jumped up, grateful for the distraction.

"Excuse me," she said, getting up from the table. She opened the side door to a young, attractive girl who appeared to be in distress. "Hi, is my Dad here?"

Donna was just about to ask who her Dad was when she heard Jim behind her. "Leah?"

Of course. His daughter. She should have known. The young woman had the same piercing blue eyes as her father. In her arms was a cat, bundled in a blanket. Donna held the door open wider and allowed the young woman to step into the hallway.

"Leah, what happened?" Jim said, rushing down the stairs.

"Hazel was hit by a car!"

"What? How?" Jim asked.

"She dashed out the door when I came home," Leah sobbed. "When I chased after her, she ran into the street and was hit by a car."

"Okay, honey, let's find where there's an emergency vet in town and we'll take Hazel there now," Jim said, taking charge.

"I'm sorry, can I interrupt?" Donna said. They both looked at her. "My son is a veterinarian. Let me call him."

"Do you think he'd mind?" Leah asked. Tears streaked her face.

"Not at all," Donna said. She pulled her phone from her pocket and waved them in. "Come into the kitchen." The girl's distress tugged at Donna's heart.

Donna indicated to Leah that she should sit down. She rang Brent, told him the situation, and hung up the phone. "Brent said to meet him at his clinic."

"He'd do that?" Leah asked in disbelief, still cradling the swaddled, injured cat.

"Of course he would," Donna said. "Will I drive you over there?" The young woman was so distraught that Donna was moved to help her.

"No, that's not necessary," Jim said. "I'll take her. Where is Brent's clinic located?"

Donna gave them directions and wished them good luck.

She returned to the gathering in her dining room to find everyone just sitting there, waiting and most likely listening to the drama in the kitchen.

"It's getting late, so let's get down to business so we can go home," Donna announced. She took her seat, picked up her pen, and went down the laundry list of things to catch up on. Once everything was ticked off, she announced that the meeting was over. She stood up and began to clear off the table to indicate that there would be no lingering.

"I guess the meeting is over," Sarge said, her tone of disapproval evident.

"I think we've covered everything," Donna said.

"We're good, Donna, see you next week," Christine said. She stood up and pulled on her coat.

Sarge lingered after the meeting. "Ralph, go outside and warm up the car."

Silently, Ralph pulled on his cap and coat, bid Donna goodnight, and went outside.

"Listen, Donna, no offense, but I think I should take over the running of the festival."

Donna pressed her lips together and regarded Sarge. For some strange reason, she was not surprised by this. If it were anyone else other than Sarge, namely someone with a better personality, she would have gladly handed over the reins. But not Sarge. She could hardly be accused of possessing a sparkling personality. If Mary Ellen had wanted Sarge to run the show, she would have asked her.

As tired as she was, Donna knew she had to proceed with caution.

"At this stage in the game, maybe we just leave it as it is," Donna said gently.

Sarge scowled. "This late in the game? You've only been in charge for a few days. Don't let the power go to your head."

Donna sighed. This was why Sarge couldn't be in charge.

"Then you should be talking to Mary Ellen and not me," Donna suggested.

"I already spoke to Mary Ellen," Sarge said.

"And what did she say?"

"To leave it as is," Sarge said.

"Then maybe we should," Donna said. Sarge appeared crestfallen. Had running the festival been an aspiration of Sarge's? A lifelong dream?

Outside, the toot of a car horn signaled Ralph was ready to leave.

Donna had an idea. "You can help, though." Actually, Donna could use some help. And if Sarge was offering, why shouldn't she accept it? "Would you be interested in being the liaison between the grammar school, the middle school, and the high school? They're all involved in some capacity. And really, there should be one person overseeing all of that. Plus, you could judge the coloring contest for the kids from the grammar school."

There was a slight lift of the corner of Sarge's mouth. Was that a smile? Donna wondered. If so, she might need to sit down.

Sarge was just about to say something when they were interrupted by the sound of a blaring horn in the driveway. Sarge turned toward the door and bellowed, "Hold your horses, Ralph, I'll be right there!" To no one in particular, she grumbled, "Get married, they said. It will be so much fun, they said."

Donna gave her the numbers of the contact people at the schools. After Sarge left, Donna didn't know if she was more relieved at the thought of help or worried about Sarge's management style. Either way, she was going to just let it play out.

Once she left, Donna loaded the dishwasher and kept watch out her window for lights to go on next door in Jim's house. She hoped the cat would be all right. Once the dishwasher was turned on, Donna shut off the kitchen lights and went to the living room.

In the corner sat a retro turntable. She'd been forced to buy one when her old stereo system just could not be repaired anymore as its parts and components were no longer manufactured. In the corner was a stack of Christmas albums. She fingered through them, choosing one of her mother's favorites.

When Donna was growing up, her mother bought a brand-new Christmas album every holiday season. Donna still had all her mother's old albums as well as her own. Between the two of them, they'd collected over thirty.

She pulled an album out of its faded jacket, laid it on the turntable, and set down the needle. The initial scratchy static never failed to make her nostalgic.

Once the music started playing, she settled on her sofa and pulled her yarn-bombing project out of her knitting bag and got to work. Every so often, she stood up to flip the album over or to change it altogether. As she did, she'd walk through to the kitchen and glance out the window to see if Jim had come home yet.

As she was heading upstairs for the night, she heard a knock on her door.

She flipped on the hall light and the outside light, relieved to see Jim standing outside.

"Come in," she said, opening the door wide and ushering him inside. She walked up into the kitchen and Jim followed her.

"How's the cat?" she asked.

Jim sighed. "She's got some internal bleeding."

"Oh no, I'm sorry to hear that," Donna said.

"When I left, Hazel was going in for emergency surgery," he said. "I just stopped at home to collect a few things for Leah, and then I'm going back to sit with her."

"Would you like some company?" she asked.

"No thanks, Donna," he said. "I just wanted to stop and say thank you. I really appreciate your help earlier."

"Not a problem, that's what neighbors are for." Donna smiled.

"I'd better get back," Jim said, and he went back outside.

"Jim," Donna called out.

He stopped and looked back at her. Donna searched his face. Worry and fatigue etched his features.

"Will you keep me posted about Hazel?"

"Sure," he said. He seemed to hesitate but added, "Goodnight, Donna."

She had wanted to talk to him, but now was not the time.

CHAPTER 8

*I*t was late by the time Jim and Leah arrived home from the vet clinic. Hazel had survived the surgery but her road to recovery would be long. Jim had been impressed by Donna's son, Brent. He'd been professional but kind and handled Hazel with care, which relieved Leah.

Once the cat was out of surgery, Brent had said the first twenty-four hours would be critical. When he told them to go home and come back in the morning, Leah had balked but Brent had explained that there'd be a tech there all night and there was no need to stay. When Leah continued her teary, ashen-faced protest, Brent gave her his business card with his cell number and home phone written on the back of it. He told her she could call him any time. Jim gently led her away, reassuring her that they were only a five-minute drive from the clinic and could be back there at any time during the night if necessary.

Leah was quiet on the drive back to Jim's house. He was pretty sure she was as tired as he was. She looked as wrecked as he felt. The past few days were starting to catch up with him. He couldn't wait to climb into bed.

After he pulled into the driveway, he ran next door to Donna's to let her know how they made out. When he returned, he found Leah in the kitchen, holding Tiny tight and cuddling him.

"Your big sister, Hazel, is going to be all right."

If the circumstances were different, Jim would have rolled his eyes. But he resisted and said, "I'm going up. I'll see you in the morning."

"Thanks, Dad," Leah said. "Handy that your next-door neighbor's son is a vet."

"Yeah, handy," he repeated absentmindedly.

"What's her name again?" Leah asked, scratching behind Tiny's ear.

"Huh?"

"The woman next door? Brent's mother?"

"Donna. Her name is Donna," he said. Exhausted, he started to walk away, but Leah was still talking.

"Are you all right?" she asked.

"Yeah, why?" he asked, rubbing the back of his head and not looking at her.

Leah shrugged. "I don't know. You don't seem yourself since I've come home."

"It's nothing."

"Are you sure? It's just that you've been more quiet than usual," Leah said.

"Am I?" he asked.

She laughed. "Yeah. I miss your blustery old self."

Even Jim had to laugh. "I'll try to be more blustery from now on."

Leah's smile disappeared. "You know, Dad, retirement is a big change. You went from a career to now having all this free time on your hands. It's a big adjustment."

Jim smiled, relieved for something else to blame it on. "You're right, it's a big adjustment. But I'll be fine. Just trying to settle in."

"Okay." She smiled. "I'm glad I'm here."

"Me, too, honey," he said truthfully, and he leaned into her and kissed her on her forehead. "Sleep well."

Jim went to bed, but once there, sleep evaded him. It hurt him to see his daughter so upset. *No matter how old she gets, what hurts her, hurts me,* he thought. *What worries her, worries me.* He was almost glad for the distraction of worrying over his daughter, as it kept his mind off of Donna.

WHEN JIM finally rolled out of bed near dawn and headed to the bathroom, he got the shock of his life.

Yawning and scratching the back of his head, he walked into the bathroom to find the cat, Tiny, standing on one side of the toilet seat, squatting over the toilet and peeing. Half awake, Jim muttered, "Sorry, didn't know anyone was in here." Then he blinked twice. "What the—" So as not to startle the cat, he stepped out of the bathroom and called, "Leah?"

Leah emerged from her bedroom in a pair of green and red Christmas pajamas, looking bleary-eyed. "What's going on?"

"I don't know, maybe you could tell me," he said. He held out his hand toward the bathroom. Leah stepped inside, saw Tiny and said, "Oh, that's Tiny. He's using the toilet."

He rolled his eyes. "I can see that," Jim said. "Doesn't he have a litter box to use?"

Leah didn't seem perturbed by this. "Of course he does, but he prefers the toilet."

"Does he at least flush when he's finished?" Jim asked.

Leah grimaced and said, "No, he hasn't mastered that yet."

"Leah, I didn't pay for your expensive college for you to spend your life potty training cats!"

Leah laughed. "I didn't train him. He taught himself." She sounded like a proud mother. Sometimes he worried about her.

"That's worse." He ignored the amused grin on his daughter's face and announced, "I need coffee to deal with this." Still laughing, Leah went back to her room to get dressed.

Later, as he sat at the table drinking his coffee and reading the paper, Tiny walked by. Jim eyed the cat suspiciously and muttered, "If he ever tells me we're out of toilet paper, he's out of here."

Leah arrived in the kitchen and glanced at the clock. "The clinic doesn't open until nine." She put her hands on her hips. "I've got ninety minutes. Why don't we start decorating the Christmas tree?"

When Jim appeared to hesitate, Leah laughed. "Okay, Dad. If you can just put the lights on, I'll do the rest."

He looked at her. "Okay."

Leah sighed. "I'm just trying to keep myself busy until the clinic opens."

"Let me finish my coffee and I'll put the lights up."

"Thanks, Dad. I'll do the rest."

Ten minutes later, Jim began untangling Christmas tree lights. Leah pulled out holiday decorations and set them up around the house. Behind them, Tiny stepped gingerly through the boxes, meowing amidst tissue paper ruffling.

Leah looked over to the cat. "Aw, he misses Hazel. Dad, would you mind giving me a ride over to the clinic so I can see how she's doing?"

"Sure, I'll drop you off. I have to go into town anyway," Jim said.

"Okay, thanks," Leah said. "We didn't hear anything from the clinic during the night, so I'm taking that as a good sign."

"Me, too, honey," Jim said reassuringly.

"If I have time today, I'll make some Christmas cookies," she said.

"That's a great idea."

"Vegan of course," she quickly added.

That meant no butter. Jim tried not to wince. "Of course," he said.

LATER WHEN JIM picked up Leah, she seemed to be in a much better mood. She emerged from the clinic smiling, and Jim breathed a sigh of relief.

As she got into his car, he asked, "How's the cat?"

Leah nodded. "She's going to be all right. It'll be a slow road but she's showing improvement."

As Jim rolled out of the clinic's parking lot, she said, "And guess what? I've got a date with that hot veterinarian!"

"He asked you out? That seems a bit unprofessional," he said, suddenly feeling protective of his daughter.

Leah laughed, amused. "Oh, Dad, it's the new millennium. I asked him out."

Jim looked over at his daughter but said nothing. He wasn't sure how he felt about her going out with Donna's son. His gut told him he didn't like it. But he kept his mouth shut for a change.

"Are you going out tonight?"

Leah shook her head. "No, the weekend. Oh, and I'm going out Christmas shopping later, so I won't be home for dinner if that's all right."

"Sure," Jim said, used to fending for himself.

JIM'S CELL PHONE RANG. Frowning, he glanced at it and saw Donna's name flash across the screen.

"Hello?"

"Jim, it's Donna."

"What's up?" he asked, unsure but curious as to the reason for her call.

She hesitated and then asked quickly, "I was wondering if you'd want to come over for dinner tonight?" Before he could respond, she said, "I know it's short notice, so if you can't, don't worry about it."

Jim smiled. "Not at all. Actually, Leah has other plans, so dinner would be great," he said, rubbing the back of his neck with his free hand. "What time?"

"Seven? Or is that too late?"

"Nope, seven is fine. See you then," he said.

"I MADE A ROAST CHICKEN. I hope that's okay," Donna said, donning oven mitts and pulling a blue enameled roasting pan out of the oven.

"Sounds great," Jim said. "Leah's a vegan so meat's off the menu for me." He removed his jacket and laid it on the chair. "Is there anything I can do?"

She nodded to a pot on the stove. "Would you mind mashing the potatoes?"

"Sure thing," he said. Jim looked into the pot of boiled potatoes, butter, and milk. He frowned. "You heat up the milk?"

Donna nodded as she transported the chicken from the pan to a platter. "Yes, it makes the potatoes starchier. I've got the electric hand mixer set up over there," she said with a nod to the mixer set up on the other side of the counter.

"No hand masher?"

She shook her head. "Not worth the hassle."

As Jim mashed the potatoes, Donna drained the carrots and set about making gravy from the pan drippings.

Once everything was ready, they sat down at the table.

"I thought it would be nicer to eat here in the kitchen since it's just the two of us," Donna said.

"It's perfect," he said. He uncorked a bottle of white wine he'd brought with him.

"Oh, I forgot the stuffing," Donna said. She stood back up, retrieved a pan, and scooped stuffing onto their plates. "You're probably wondering why I invited you over to dinner."

"It may have crossed my mind," Jim said, taking the gravy boat and pouring gravy over his potatoes.

"I've been doing a lot of thinking lately," Donna admitted. "Well, to be more precise, since the issue of the letter came up."

"You're not the only one," Jim said, putting a forkful of chicken and mashed potatoes into his mouth. "This is delicious, by the way."

"Jim, we're not teenagers anymore and I'd prefer to be upfront and honest with you," she said.

"Okay," he said cautiously. "I appreciate that."

"First, can I ask what you wrote in that letter? Other than the proposal?" she asked.

Jim nodded as he finished chewing. "I don't remember it verbatim but I do recall the gist of it. I said I'd made a huge mistake in breaking up with you. I asked for forgiveness. I said that I could handle anything including war but what I could not handle was us not being together. I asked you to marry me. And since I ruined your Christmas, I promised to make it up to you the following Christmas and all the Christmases thereafter."

"Oh," Donna said.

They were quiet for a few minutes as they let this settle.

"I admit to there being a bit of residual anger over you

dumping me all those years ago, but that's gone now. When I first saw you, it was my twenty-year-old hurt self that reacted to you and your presence in Orchard Falls. I did not react from the perspective of the woman I am today," she said.

She paused and Jim waited. He was perfectly happy to let her speak while he listened and enjoyed a roast chicken dinner.

"I think we need to make peace with the fact that had that letter arrived, our lives would have turned out very differently," she said.

"Agreed," he said.

"But that letter didn't arrive, and here we are, with our lives as we know them because of it."

"But no matter how things had ended up, I always planned to retire to Orchard Falls," he said. "I'll be the first to admit, though, that that's been a bit of a challenge."

"Really?" she asked.

"Yes. I'm happy to be back, but I'm still not sure where I fit in," he explained. "I've been gone so long I wondered if coming back was a mistake. That maybe the old saying, 'You can never go home again,' was true for me."

"Do you still feel that way?" Donna asked, her eyes never leaving his face.

"If I'm honest, yes, I do," Jim said. He struggled to get the right words together. It was important for her to know exactly how he felt. He was leaving nothing to chance or worse, misinterpretation. "But I am working on trying to fit in here."

"Good," she said with an encouraging smile.

Jim helped Donna clear the plates and they sat back down, letting their food digest and waiting for the coffee.

"I've made peace with this lost letter and I hope you will, too," Donna said. "Of course, it changes my perspective of the past."

"The letter has become an annotated asterisk on our history?" he asked.

"More like a footnote."

"You were really angry with me," Jim said quietly.

"I was," she said. "But not anymore."

"You're very philosophical about it," he noted.

She shrugged her shoulders. "Maybe. Or maybe it's time to let the past rest." She looked at her cup on the table. "I just feel that everything worked out the way it was supposed to. At that particular point in time, for whatever reason, we were not meant to be together."

Jim dared to ask, "And what about this point in time?"

"I don't know the answer to that yet. But I would be willing . . ." her voice trailed off.

Jim leaned forward in his chair, hopeful. He helped her fill in the blanks. "To hang out? To become friends? Dare I ask it—to go out together?"

She nodded with a laugh.

"I'm interested in starting right here, right now with you," he said, thumping his forefinger on the table.

"You are?" she asked, her eyes lighting up.

"I am."

She smiled. "I like the sound of that."

"Good," Jim said. He wondered if she knew how beautiful she was to him even now, a little older, with a little extra weight and those fine lines on her face. She was more beautiful to him now than she had been at eighteen.

"Why the sudden change in heart?" he asked.

She appeared thoughtful for a moment. "My husband died unexpectedly at the age of thirty-four."

Jim shook his head. "That's rough, I'm sorry."

She gave him a small smile. "The one thing I took away from

all of that was that you have to live in the moment—because that's all we have."

A slow smile emerged on his face. "So, what are we?"

"What do you mean?" Donna asked.

"Going forward, I don't want any ambiguities. How would we define our relationship? Friends, neighbors, dating, boyfriend-girlfriend, or all of the above?"

Donna gave him a small smile and said, "It's complicated?"

Jim burst out laughing. Oh yeah, he was going to love hanging out with Donna.

RESTLESSNESS CONSUMED Jim as he thought about the conversation that had taken place earlier in the evening with Donna. He was as excited as a kid on Christmas Eve. Late that night, when he couldn't sleep, he found himself getting dressed and going for a walk, thinking the cold night air would help to settle his mind. As he headed down Main Street to the outskirts of town, something caught his eye at the underpass to the thruway. There was a gathering of people. He glanced at his watch and saw that it was just before midnight.

With a bit of hesitation, Jim walked toward the group to investigate. The last thing he wanted to do was to stumble onto a gang, but he wasn't truly afraid. He didn't think there was any gang activity in Orchard Falls.

As he neared the gathering, he slowed his pace as he eyed the situation. A group of men stood behind a long folding table, doling out food in bowls to a line of people. As Jim got closer, he saw in the line what appeared to be homeless people. They held Styrofoam bowls and plastic spoons in their hands as men behind the table doled out soup and bottles of water. Jim scanned the environment. Beneath the underpass, at the top of the embankment, he could see sleeping bags and cardboard boxes tucked against the concrete.

A thickness invaded his throat and he tried swallowing to dislodge it. How had he not known that Orchard Falls had a homeless population? He drove through this underpass at least once a week and he had never noticed people sleeping rough beneath it, vying for protection from the elements.

Curious, he walked toward the group. As he approached the table, the men behind it gave him a slight nod of acknowledgement. There was a small line of people—mainly men but some women—lined up with bowls in their hands. They wore layers of clothing. They did not make eye contact with Jim.

Uncomfortable with standing around and doing nothing, Jim asked the guy at the end of the table nearest him, "Anything I can do to help?"

"Hold on." The man, in his seventies, turned around and called to another man unloading boxes from the back of a van. "Bob?" When the other man looked toward him, he nodded his head toward Jim.

Bob walked over. He was a heavyset man wearing a hoodie, a knit cap, and a winter jacket. "What can I do for you?"

Jim smiled and looked around at the setup. "More like what can I do to help?"

"As you can see, we offer something hot to eat on cold nights. Soup, chili, stews, whatever we get from our volunteer cooks. In the summertime, we give out sandwiches and popsicles on the real hot nights."

Jim raised an eyebrow, impressed. "I'm ashamed to admit I didn't know that there were homeless people in Orchard Falls."

Bob nodded. "Most people don't. It isn't addressed too much."

"It's a little cold out here. Is there a shelter they could go to?" Jim asked.

Bob shook his head. "We don't have a purpose-built shelter as of yet. Right now, the church lets us use their parish hall on the really cold nights—when the mercury drops below freezing."

Jim tried to process all this information. And he knew immediately that he wanted to be involved. "And you're here every night?"

"We are. Rain or shine. No matter what the weather. Weekends. Holidays."

"Do you need help?"

"We always need help. What can you do?"

"Anything," Jim said. "I can do anything you ask me."

"That's good to know. Give me your number and I'll be in touch," Bob said.

Jim took out his phone and rattled off his number.

"If you want to help tonight, you can take Ernie's place behind the table," Bob suggested. "Ernie has to run back to his house and get more soup. On the colder nights, we have bigger crowds."

"Of course." Jim took over from Ernie and began doling out soup to the people in line. The soup smelled good. Steam rose off of it, and Jim saw that it was heavy with noodles and vegetables and pieces of chicken.

Within the hour, they were all finished and Jim helped with the cleanup. He told them he'd be back the next night. As he walked home, his head held high, he whistled, feeling better than he had in a long time. He was a good kind of tired.

CHAPTER 9

*D*onna sat in her office with Tim and Dottie Fields. This was one of those days that reminded Donna how much she loved her job. Tim and Dottie had been loyal customers almost as long as Donna had been with the bank. They hadn't always had it easy. In the past, Tim had been laid off from the plant and there were many years of unemployment, and Dottie had only a high-school education, but they'd managed to scrimp and save, raise four children, and send them all to college.

Out of the blue, they'd received a large and unexpected windfall. A distant relative of Dottie's had passed away and left Dottie her entire estate. Nobody had been more shocked than Dottie. And no one deserved it more, thought Donna. They were good people. Over the decades, Donna had been behind Dottie in line more than once at the grocery store and it was always the same thing: lots of coupons and generic-brand items. They had one old car that they shared, and there was nothing flashy about them. Donna didn't think much would change, despite the huge windfall. Frugality born of necessity sometimes became an ingrained habit.

"As excited as we are about this money, we want to be careful with it," Dottie said. "We're not going to go out and buy a new car or anything like that. But we are going to treat ourselves to a dishwasher." Her husband smiled at her.

They'd all gone to high school together. Dottie and Tim had also been high-school sweethearts. But unlike them, Tim hadn't left town, and there was no lost letter to upend their lives. As Donna listened to their chatter, she thought that this was what it would be like to have spent decades with the man you loved, and to finally be getting to the good times. To have all that common history and time together, behind you and a part of you. A lump formed in her throat.

Her thoughts drifted toward Jim, as they always seemed to be doing lately. She was glad he'd come for dinner. She was happy about their agreement but at the same time, she wanted to keep it to herself. It felt special to her.

Once she went over in detail some proper investment vehicles for the Fieldses, she gave them some literature to look over and penned in a follow-up appointment in her diary.

They'd no sooner left than her cell phone rang.

"Hi, honey," she answered when Brent's name flashed across the screen.

"Hey, Mom, I'm just calling to let you know that I won't be able to make dinner tonight," he explained.

"Are you working late again?" she asked, trying to keep the worry out of her voice.

Brent laughed. "Actually, I have a date."

Donna perked up and hope filled her. "You do? That's wonderful! With who?"

"With Leah O'Hara, your neighbor's daughter," Brent said. "You know, the one whose cat got run over the other night."

Donna sank back in her executive chair. "I know who you mean."

"I thought you'd be happy," Brent said.

"Oh, happy isn't the word," Donna said truthfully.

"I've got to go; my next appointment's here," Brent said. "I'll talk to you later."

"Bye, Brent." Donna stared at her phone for a solid minute.

Brent going out on a date with Jim's daughter was not a good idea. How on earth would she tell her son that his mother had a significant history with his date's father? How would she explain that Jim O'Hara had been her great love before Brent's father?

It was only one date, she reminded herself. And Leah lived in another state. There wouldn't be enough time for them to get involved. Just two young people making the most of the holidays. It might be casual, but it also might be just the sort of thing Brent needed.

Maybe she wouldn't have to say anything at all.

WHEN DONNA ARRIVED home from work and parked her car in her garage, Jim walked over. The sight of him—the rugged physique and his impossible height—made her heart skip a beat. He still ticked all the boxes for her.

"I just wanted to let you know that the cat is going to be all right," Jim said.

"I'm glad to hear it," she said. "Is she still at the clinic?"

"Yes, for another day or two," Jim replied. "I can't thank your son enough for helping Leah out after hours. I'm sure he has better things to do after he gets off work."

Donna didn't say anything about the fact that Brent had nothing to do after work. That work, his clinic, and the animals were his life.

She smiled. "That's Brent. He's always happy to help."

"He's a credit to you, Donna," Jim said.

It was beginning to darken outside. Up and down the street,

houses were bejeweled in colorful Christmas lights, lending a feel of merriment to the atmosphere.

"Thank you," she said. "Did you want to come in? Have something to drink?"

"I would love to, but Mr. Brenneman invited me to his poker game," Jim said.

Donna grinned. "Don't lose your shirt." As soon as she said it, an image of him shirtless came to mind and she blushed. As if he were reading her mind, Jim raised one eyebrow and grinned.

Jim changed the subject. "Leah and Brent are going out tonight."

"I heard that," Donna said. "Are you okay with it?"

"Sure," Jim said.

"Have you told Leah about us?"

Jim shook his head.

"I haven't said anything to Brent, either. Maybe we don't have to say anything right away," Donna said. There was no point in telling them their history if it only turned out to be one date.

"All right."

"Okay, then, goodnight, Jim," Donna said.

"I'll call you tomorrow."

———

DONNA DID NOT SLEEP WELL that night. Finally, at one in the morning, she gave it up and got out of bed. She was no stranger to infrequent bouts of insomnia. When she'd gone through menopause, she'd suffered terribly from sleeplessness. A few nights a week for one solid year. She supposed it could have been worse. At least she'd never had one of those awful hot flashes that Christine used to complain about. She'd discovered the best cure was to get out of bed and do something for an hour. Donna usually did housework.

As she folded laundry at her kitchen table, Donna saw a text flash across her screen. Jim.

Why are your lights on?

She typed a quick reply. *Because I can't see in the dark.*

His response was swift. *I mean why are you up at this hour of the night?*

I can't sleep. Why are you up?

Out walking. Just came home. What are you doing?

Housework, she responded and thought it sounded lame.

Can I come over?

Oh no! she thought. Why would he want to come over in the middle of the night?

Before she could give it too much thought, she texted an "okay" back to him.

Mumbling, Donna ran to the downstairs bathroom. She splashed some cold water on her face and pinched her cheeks to give them a rosy glow. Then she gave her teeth a quick brush with a spare toothbrush she kept in the vanity. She ran to her kitchen window and saw his porch light turn on and the door open. He really was coming over! The fool. She looked down at what she was wearing: a pair of striped pajamas and a big, burly housecoat that had outlived its attractiveness but still remained functional and cozy. Her hair was pinned back and she wore glasses. She was not putting on any make-up.

There was a sharp knock on her side door. She opened it and let him in. A blast of cold air blew in with him and Donna pulled her bathrobe around her tighter, shivering. Jim stamped the snow off his boots and followed her into the kitchen. She laughed when she saw that Jim had thrown his winter coat on over a long-sleeved thermal top and a pair of pajama bottoms.

Jim frowned and said, "You look hot, Donna."

Donna blushed and her pulse quickened. "Jim."

His mouth opened and he said, "No, I meant your cheeks are pink, like you're too warm or something."

Donna reddened further and pulled her bathrobe closed at the neck and said, "Oh, oh."

Jim took in the sight of her, raised an eyebrow, and smiled. "I see you're still irresistible, Donna."

Donna tilted her head and regarded him with a smirk. "I dress for comfort now, Jim."

"Like I said, you're irresistible."

Donna didn't know if he was teasing her or not. His tone said he was, but his lingering gaze said otherwise.

"How was your poker game?" she asked.

He laughed. "I lost my shirt." He looked around her kitchen. "I had to come over and see for myself. You're doing housework in the middle of the night? Why?"

She shrugged. "When I can't sleep, I get up and do housework for an hour. Then I'm tired enough to go back to bed."

"I'll have to try it," he said.

"Housework?" she asked, surprised. "Your mother couldn't get you to make your bed."

"It's been a long time since I was seventeen."

She snorted. "You and me both. Would you like a mug of hot chocolate?" She looked at him and added, "Or would you like something stronger?"

"Do you make hot chocolate the way your mother used to make it?" he asked, cocking one eyebrow.

Her features softened. "You remember."

"Best hot chocolate ever," he said. "How could I forget?"

"Yes, I make it like my mother used to," she said.

"Then that's what I'll have."

Without another word, Donna pulled a small saucepan out from the bottom cabinet and set it on the stove. She pulled out milk, cocoa, and vanilla and set them on the countertop. She was aware of Jim's eyes on her as she added the ingredients to the pot.

"I wonder how the date went with Brent and Leah," Donna said as she stirred the cocoa in the pot with a wooden spoon.

Jim shrugged. "I didn't see Leah come in." He paused and asked. "Is that what kept you up?"

"I suppose," she said.

"We're probably worrying about nothing," Jim said. "It may be only one date."

"Where does your daughter live?" Donna asked.

"She lives in California, near Carol," Jim said.

"What does she do?"

"She trains guide dogs for the blind," he answered proudly.

"That's wonderful."

"Leah was a dual major in college: biology and communications, but I always knew she'd work with animals."

Another animal lover. Donna hoped Brent wouldn't get hurt if he continued to go out with Leah. With her living on the other side of the country, it would be hard to have a relationship with her. Donna's son didn't rebound easily from lost relationships. He'd been crushed when his father had died. *It's just one date,* she told herself. *Stop worrying.*

Once the hot chocolate was ready, Donna poured it into two mugs and added a little milk and a dollop of whipped cream.

"Would you like marshmallows?"

Jim smiled. "No, thanks. I gave up my marshmallow habit back in the fourth grade."

She grabbed a few mini-marshmallows and sprinkled them on top of her own mug. When she handed him his hot chocolate, he was grinning.

"What? I still like marshmallows in mine," she said.

"Hey, that's okay," he said, taking a sip. He looked up and smiled at her. "It's as delicious as I remember."

She nodded a thanks and spooned up some whipped cream and marshmallows into her mouth.

"I wonder how their date went," Donna mused.

Jim laughed. "Leah's a talker. Hopefully Brent will be able to get a word in."

Donna smiled and sipped her hot chocolate. "Brent is reserved and doesn't say much."

Jim lifted an eyebrow. "Opposites attract?"

She tilted her head slightly and regarded him. "Maybe."

"How does their dating affect us?" Jim asked.

"I've thought about this," she admitted. "And I don't want whatever happens between them to affect us. We've got a fresh start and the last thing we need is any drama."

"Agreed."

"And if it should by some chance work out between them, then that's great."

Jim nodded.

They sipped their beverages in silence for a few moments.

It was Jim who spoke first. "You know it may be just the two of them enjoying the holidays together and each other's company."

"Right. And no matter what happens, it can't affect us."

Jim grinned. "You seem very protective of our relationship."

Donna blushed. "Maybe I am."

"Me, too, if I'm honest," Jim said softly. They sat for a few minutes in companionable silence. He finished the rest of his hot chocolate in one gulp and stood up. "It's almost two and I've kept you up long enough."

Jim set his empty mug in the sink and headed out the door, pulling on his coat as he went.

"Wait a minute, Jim," Donna called out.

Jim stood there, holding the storm door open. "Yes?"

"You never told me what I owed you for the quart of candy cane ice cream," she said.

He paused and appeared thoughtful. Finally, he grinned, "One kiss. That's what you owe me, Donna St. James. One kiss for Christmas."

Donna stood there for a long time after he'd left, staring at the door.

One kiss. That's all he wanted.

*a*t first, Jim really hadn't thought there would be any need to tell Leah or Brent that he and Donna had significant history together or that they were trying to make a fresh start. But that was before Leah went out every night that week with Brent. They'd gone ice skating, to the movies, to dinner, and one night they'd gone tobogganing with friends of Brent's. Leah seemed happy, and that's what worried Jim. Brent could be the nicest guy in the world, and he probably was no doubt, but the fact of the matter was that Leah lived in California and Brent had a fledgling veterinary practice here in Orchard Falls on the other side of the country. It was hard to see how it could work out. And being a veteran of a disastrous, life-altering long-distance relationship, it was something he felt strongly about. He didn't want to see either one of them get hurt.

One evening before Leah was due to meet Brent at the mall to do some Christmas shopping, Jim decided he'd have a quick chat with his daughter. It must be leaning toward serious if Brent was accompanying Leah to go shopping, he thought. Jim would rather stick hot pokers in his eyes than go to a mall. Thank goodness for online shopping.

"It seems to be getting pretty serious with the vet," Jim said as Leah stood in the kitchen, bundling up in her scarf and coat.

"His name is Brent," Leah said with a smirk. "And you know that."

"Okay," he conceded. "It's just that you've been out with him every night this week."

"Dad." She slung the strap of her purse over her shoulder.

"I'm just saying, honey. You'll be going home right after Christmas and I'd hate to see either one of you get hurt."

"We'll be fine," Leah said. "Brent knows this is short-term." She gave him a smile and said pointedly, "*I* know it's short-term. We're just keeping each other company over the holidays."

Still not satisfied, he decided to drop it. He changed tact. "Has Brent ever talked about his mother?" He eyed her nervously.

Leah pulled on a glove and frowned. "In what way?"

Jim shrugged. "I don't know."

Leah broke into a smile. "Do you want us to play matchmaker? Has the lovely Mrs. St. James caught your eye?" Leah joked. "Dad, you dog!"

"No, it isn't anything like that," Jim said before adding defiantly, "and if it was, I certainly wouldn't need a matchmaker."

"Then what do you mean?" Leah asked.

"I was just wondering if Brent ever mentioned that his mother and I used to know each other," he said.

Leah frowned again. "As in, you went to school together?"

"It was a little more complicated than that," Jim said.

"A little more complicated? You better explain yourself," Leah said, standing still and making no moves to depart.

Not for the first time, Jim wondered who the parent was. "Actually, we were high-school sweethearts."

Leah stared at him with her mouth hanging open. "Was it serious?"

Jim nodded. "It was."

Leah sank down in a chair, the date with Brent momentarily forgotten. "What happened?"

Jim certainly wasn't going to get into the details. "I went off to college then off to war, and we drifted apart," he explained, giving her a heavily edited and condensed version.

Leah looked at him evenly. "You mean she dumped you?"

"No, I don't mean that at all. It just didn't work out."

"Huh," Leah said to no one in particular.

"Yeah," Jim said. He glanced at the clock. "You better get going; you don't want to be late."

Leah stood up, leaned over, and kissed her father on the cheek. "Goodnight, Dad. Don't wait up for me."

Jim's thoughts were interrupted by his ringing phone. Not recognizing the number, he answered it, curious.

As Jim walked home later that evening after helping out at the soup table, he thought about the phone call he'd received from his old army buddy. By the end of that phone call, Jim had received an offer for the position of managing director for a security firm out in California. He'd told his friend he'd think about it. A little frisson of excitement gripped him at the thought of a new challenge. But Donna immediately came to mind. As much as California excited him—he would at least be in the same state as his daughter—he wanted to give Orchard Falls a chance.

When he walked up his driveway, he saw the lights on over at Donna's house. She must be having another bout of insomnia, he thought.

Once inside, he locked the door and hung up his coat. He texted Donna.

What are you cleaning now?

It was few minutes before she responded, *Cleaning out cupboards.*

Can I call you? he typed.

Immediately, she sent back, *Yes.*

Jim poured himself a glass of orange juice, picked up the receiver off the wall phone, dialed, and sat down at the kitchen table, the coiled cord of the phone stretching across the room from the wall to the table.

"Hi, Jim, how are you?" Donna asked.

"I'm well. Insomnia again?" he asked.

"Unfortunately. But I'm getting a lot done," she said.

"Yeah, but you're going to be wrecked tomorrow at work," he said.

"I know. But that's the way it is. I'll just have to soldier through," Donna said.

"So Donna . . ." Jim told her about the job offer in California. He could practically hear her surprise over the line.

She went silent for a moment, then asked, "Are you seriously considering it?"

"I don't know. Maybe in a plan-B type of way. Like if it didn't work out here in Orchard Falls," he admitted.

"I appreciate you telling me this," she said quietly.

"If we're going to be friends... or whatever, then no secrets," he said.

"I agree," she said. There was silence on the line for a moment before Donna spoke again. "Can I call you back in ten minutes?"

Frowning, he said, "Sure." They hung up, and he wondered if she would call back. He looked at the clock and saw it was almost one thirty in the morning. He rinsed his glass out and laid it on the top rack of the dishwasher. As he glanced out his kitchen window, he saw the lights go out downstairs in Donna's house. Was she going back to bed?

Starting to feel a little tired, he headed up to his room and got ready for bed. He was just slipping under the bedcovers when his phone on the nightstand rang. He lifted it up on the first ring, hoping it hadn't woken Leah. "Sorry about that," Donna said.

"Have you gone to bed?" Jim asked, getting his own head comfortable on the pillow.

"Uh . . . yeah," Donna stuttered. "I am in bed."

Jim chuckled. "Just like old times." During high school, they used to talk on the phone at night until one of them fell asleep.

"I guess so," Donna said softly. "Do you want to go to bed and we could talk?"

"I'm already there."

"Oh, Jim." Donna laughed. "Okay, now let me ask you a question: I see you go out walking at night, and I was wondering why you walk so late," Donna said.

He was impressed that she knew his routine. "I like to take a walk to clear my head before going to bed." He paused and asked, "Did you know that there are homeless people in Orchard Falls?"

"What?" she asked with the same tone of disbelief he'd felt when he'd seen it firsthand.

"I'm only just finding this out myself," he admitted. He launched into his discovery of the little impromptu soup table at the side of the road by the underpass. Donna was shocked. He told her how he'd joined the team of volunteers. "But giving someone a hot bowl of soup doesn't seem like enough."

"It's a start, though," Donna said.

"I just feel I could be doing more," he said.

"Like what?"

"I don't know yet. I've been thinking about it."

They batted ideas back and forth until Jim heard Donna yawn on the other end of the line. He glanced at the bedside clock and saw that it was nearing three.

"Donna, you have to get to sleep. It's getting late," he said.

She laughed. "Is that an order?"

"Yes, it is," he said.

They said their goodnights and hung up.

With his hands clasped behind his head, Jim stared at the ceiling for a long time, thinking. Thinking about Donna, the job offer, the homeless . . . but most of all about Donna.

CHAPTER 11

"Okay, Christine, so where are we with the ice sculptures?" Donna asked at the weekly meeting for the Snowball Festival.

"It's a go," Christine said. "I've spoken to the guy who's donating them, and they're ready for pickup. I've made arrangements for their transportation, and they'll be here Friday evening by five for the outdoor festivities."

"That's great," Donna said.

The Snowball Festival would start Friday night at six and wrap up with the dance, the Snow Ball, on Sunday night. It was a weekend-long extravaganza.

Donna scribbled some notes on a legal pad. She looked up at Sarge, who sat across from her at the dining-room table. "Sarge, what about the schools?" Donna asked.

"I've spoken to the elementary school, and the principal assures me that the younger grades are working diligently on their coloring and will have their posters ready by Thursday," Sarge said.

"And when are you judging the coloring contest?"

"I've already arranged with the school that I'll go through all the posters on Thursday and pick a winner. We can announce the winner on Saturday because most families will be there in the afternoon for the craft fair. That way the winners could be on display," Sarge replied.

Donna nodded. "That sounds good." She penned down more notes and asked, "And what about the older grades?"

"I'm on it," Sarge said, referring to her own notes. "The middle school is all ready for the craft fair, with the proceeds going toward their trip next year."

"Perfect," Donna said. Everyone at the table murmured approval.

"But I told them the crafts have to get my approval," Sarge said firmly. "We don't want any junk."

Donna tried not to grimace. From across the table, Jim gave her a stare as if he was trying not to laugh.

"Let's remember, they're middle-school children, so the crafts are going to be very . . . homemade-looking," Donna said gently, hoping Sarge would take the hint.

"Yeah, like I said, we don't want any junk."

Donna tried again. "Let's give them a lot of leeway." Ignoring Sarge's frown, she added, "In the spirit of the holidays and all of that. They must be so excited about their trip." She paused and added, "And what about the high school?"

"I spoke to the art department and they plan on doing some type of winter wonderland sets for indoors," Sarge said. "I told her to make sure the paint is dry before they assemble it. We don't want paint all over the floor like last year. It cost us a bomb to get the floor professionally cleaned after that debacle." More scowling from Sarge. "And I told her no glitter. We're always finding Christmas glitter at the Independence Day Festival."

"A little glitter is fine," Donna said.

"It makes everything look so sparkly! I think it adds a festive air," Christine piped in.

Sarge didn't say anything. She just sighed heavily, letting everyone at the table know of her displeasure.

Donna reported on the status of the knitting group's effort for the yarn bombing of Main Street.

When she was finished, she looked over to Jim and enquired about the status of the interior lighting for the community center.

"We're still waiting for the delivery. Apparently, they're coming from China."

"So, a slow boat from China?" she asked with a laugh. He laughed too.

"It would seem so."

"Keep me posted," Donna said. More notes to write.

Jim nodded. "Mr. Brenneman assured me that they'd get here in time."

"Okay, good."

Donna had had to stop herself from looking at Jim too often throughout the evening. She didn't want to come across as favoring anyone in particular. She was really enjoying the time they were spending together. Sometimes, she felt pulled by those bright blue eyes of his. They were like a magnet. It had occurred to her more than once that she might like to be more than friends with him.

The group spent the next half hour discussing what needed to be done for the Snow Ball. Everything seemed to be falling into place. Somehow, Ralph had managed to source a giant, lighted snowball that would hang suspended from the ceiling over the dance floor. When the meeting finally broke up, Jim lingered behind, helping Donna clean up.

Jim wore a heavy cable-knit sweater and a pair of jeans that hugged his muscular form. When he leaned in to load plates in the dishwasher, Donna got a hint of his cologne and as unobtrusively as possible, she closed her eyes and breathed in.

Once everything was cleared up, Jim said, "I should head

home and let you get to bed." But he seemed in no hurry to put his coat on. They stood there for a moment, looking at each other, and finally Donna laughed.

"What's wrong?" she asked.

"I'm trying to get up the nerve to ask you a question."

"Come on, Jim, you were never afraid of anything," she pointed out with raised eyebrows.

"Donna, all men are afraid of rejection."

"You're not going to ask me to marry you, are you?" she joked.

Even he had to laugh. "No, but if I ever do, I won't do it in a letter."

They both laughed and Donna thought they must be making progress if they could joke about that lost letter.

"I wanted to know if you would go to the dance with me." he asked.

"As a date?" she asked. He looked so nervous asking her that she was touched.

His Adam's apple bobbed as he swallowed hard. "Maybe as a date. What do you think?"

Donna smiled to reassure him and said quietly, "I'd really like that."

"I don't want to rush you into anything."

"I appreciate that. You know, as we're getting to know each other again, I would be okay with a date once in a while."

"You would?" he asked, surprised.

She nodded. "As long as we take things slow."

Jim smiled. It was a smile that reached his eyes, and suddenly his composure relaxed. "I can live with this." It wasn't lost on Donna that *she* had put that smile on his face and that the air around them had become charged.

He said goodnight, and Donna locked her door behind him. Once he reached his own side door, she headed upstairs. As she got ready for bed, she hummed a Christmas tune. She had to admit to a feeling of excitement about going to the dance as Jim's date. She'd been a widow for more than fifteen years, and she felt ready to move on with her personal life.

There was a television in her bedroom, and she thought she'd watch a Christmas movie from her burgeoning collection. But as she slid into bed, her phone beeped. She saw that it was Jim, and she smiled as she opened his text.

Told Leah we used to date.

Then: *Didn't mention lost letter.*

Donna exhaled a loud breath and set the phone down on her lap. She had said nothing to Brent. She turned her attention back to the movie but couldn't focus. Finally, she typed a reply: *They seem to be seeing a lot of each other.*

Jim's reply was swift. *Yes.*

Donna typed furiously. *R u ok with it?*

Jim's response: *Yes. R u?*

Donna replied, *Yes. Brent seems happy.*

Jim sent, *Leah, too.*

Donna settled into bed, thinking about Brent and Leah. At least for today, her son had found someone and was happy.

Her thoughts drifted toward Jim and she couldn't help but smile. This new arrangement between them suited her perfectly. There was only one problem. She was falling in love with Jim. Again. And he might be leaving Orchard Falls. Again.

CHAPTER 12

*J*im was greeted at Steve's front door with a slap on his back and a smile from his old friend. Something smelled good and Jim was hungry. The house was all decorated for Christmas, making it feel cozy. There was a candle burning on a small table, giving off a pleasant pine scent. Steve's wife, Lynn, came out from the kitchen. She hugged Jim.

"Dinner will be ready in fifteen minutes."

Jim handed her a bottle of wine and a box of chocolates.

"How nice, thanks, Jim," she said.

Steve took Jim's coat and they headed into the living room where they sat down. Steve offered him a drink, but Jim refused.

Steve's oldest son, Kyle, entered the room. He favored his father in his looks. Jim introduced himself and shook Kyle's hand. The boy's hand was damp and he kept wiping his hands on his pant legs.

"Nice to meet you, sir," Kyle said.

"Just call me Jim," he said, trying to put him at ease.

"Okay, Mr. O'Hara."

Steve laughed. "At ease, Kyle."

Kyle looked at his father and reddened, but he smiled. The

three of them sat there for a while making small talk. Jim asked him how school was and what his hobbies were and if he had a girlfriend. Kyle blushed at the final question and said no.

"So, you're thinking of going into the service," Jim started.

Kyle nodded. "Since I was a little boy."

"Good for you," Jim said. He remembered the guidance counselor giving him encouragement back in high school. "Is it your plan to make a career out of it?"

Kyle nodded. "I'd like to."

"Good. That's great. And do you plan to go to college or are you going right into the service?"

"I want to join as soon as I graduate," Kyle said.

Jim remembered how he felt at that age. All that restless energy, like he couldn't wait for something to happen, for his life to begin.

"If you plan on making a career out of the military, I would suggest getting a college degree first, and then you'd go into the military as an officer."

"That's how Jim did it," Steve piped in. "When he retired, he was a high-ranking career officer." Steve looked at Jim and said, "You were a full colonel when you retired, weren't you?"

Jim nodded. "I was."

Steve turned toward his son. "Higher rank means higher pay."

Kyle's eyes lit up.

"You have to ask yourself one question: do you want to be taking the orders or giving them?" Jim said.

"The way you boss your younger brothers around should give you a general idea," Steve said to his son.

Even Kyle relaxed and laughed. "But I could join the military and go to college afterward, and college would be paid for."

"That's right. The GI bill," Jim said.

They talked for a few more minutes, and Jim gave Kyle his cell number and told him to call him any time.

After dinner, Jim retreated to the basement with Steve. It was finished off with paneled walls and carpeting. There was a pool table, a ping-pong table, and a bar. There was a dartboard on the wall. In the corner, on a table, was a small Christmas tree laden with ornaments and garland and lights.

Jim glanced at it. "Nice tree for your man cave."

Steve laughed. "I can't get away from it. Lynn loves Christmas. She put that up, said the place needed some festive cheer."

Steve set up the billiard balls on the pool table and handed Jim a pool cue.

After a few rounds, Jim said, "Leah is going out with Donna's son, Brent."

Steve looked up. "The vet?"

"Yes. They went out every night last week, and this week looks to be a repeat of last week."

"Does Leah know about your past with Donna?" Steve said, rubbing blue chalk on the tip of his pool cue.

"Yeah, she does," Jim said.

"How do you feel about it?" Steve asked.

"It's awkward because it's Donna's son. But he's a decent guy, so I can't complain," Jim said. A flashback to Leah's college boyfriend came to mind. He'd appeared to have it all going on with his career path and nice clothes, but he turned out to be a jerk. Jim was just glad she didn't end up marrying the guy.

Steve looked at him. "There's a rumor going around that you and Donna are back together."

"We're spending some time together," Jim explained.

Steve grinned. "Hanging out."

Jim changed the subject, feeling protective of his fledgling relationship with Donna.

"An army buddy of mine got in touch with me last week. He retired about ten years ago. He owns this security company out in California and he's offered me the job of Managing Director."

Steve straightened up from the pool table. "In California?"

Jim nodded, leaning on his cue.

"Are you seriously thinking about it?"

"I'm not discounting it," Jim said quietly.

"What does this job have to offer that is so enticing you'd leave retirement?" Steve asked.

Jim didn't have to think about it. "I thought it might get me focused. I was really looking forward to retirement, but I still don't feel like I've found my way. And Orchard Falls isn't how I remembered it."

Steve laughed. "Come on, man, you've been gone over thirty years. Even a place like Orchard Falls is bound to change in that length of time."

"Maybe it's true that you can't go home again." Jim sighed.

"Don't say that," Steve said. "You know, when my Dad died, I was thinking of moving away from Orchard Falls."

"You were? Really?"

"Yeah, Mom was gone, and everywhere I looked in Orchard Falls reminded me of Dad. It was painful. I was chomping at the bit to get out and actually looked into selling my store and heading south or west."

"What changed your mind?" Jim asked.

Steve laughed. "Actually, Mr. Brenneman did."

"Really?"

Steve nodded. "Really. It was about three months after my Dad died, and I went into the hardware store for something and started talking to Mr. Brenneman and told him about my plans. He gave me a piece of advice that has always stayed with me. He told me not to make any major life decisions for twelve months, because grief can do funny things to our minds." Steve smiled at the memory of it. "And you know, a year after my father's death, I no longer wanted to leave Orchard Falls. Because everywhere I went, it still reminded me of my Dad, but with the passage of time, the memories weren't painful but comforting. Looking back, I'm glad I didn't go."

Jim thought about what his friend had said. "But I'm not grieving."

"No, but you are transitioning from one phase of your life to another," Steve said. "Give yourself a year here. Give yourself and Orchard Falls a chance before you make any major life decisions. No matter where you move to, you bring your issues and problems with you."

"You just don't want me to leave because then you'll have no friends left," Jim teased, trying to lighten a heavy moment.

Steve replied. "Well, there it is. Come on, cue up."

JIM COULDN'T IDENTIFY anything on his plate. Despite this, it tasted good.

Leah sat across from him. She'd cooked them a vegan dinner. Some specialty dish. She'd already told him the name twice, but he couldn't remember and he didn't dare ask a third time.

"Aren't you doing something with Brent tonight?" Jim asked.

"I'm going over to his house later. We're going to bake vegan cinnamon rolls." She drank some water. "But I thought we'd have dinner together tonight. I don't want you to feel abandoned."

"Don't worry about me, honey. You just enjoy yourself." Jim was used to eating dinner alone and it didn't bother him.

"I know, but still," she said with uncertainty.

"Do you like this guy?" he asked.

Immediately she perked up. Sat up straighter in her chair and smiled. "I do, I really do. He's so different than any other guy I've met."

Jim listened, hoping his daughter wouldn't end up with a broken heart.

"Remember what Gram used to say—about people being the genuine article? That's Brent."

"What's going to happen after you go home?" Jim asked. He helped himself to more of the casserole from the pot in the middle of the table.

"We've talked about that," Leah said. "We're going to try a long-distance relationship when I return to California. Brent said he's had no vacation since he opened his clinic. Said he'd like to come out to California in February or March."

Jim sighed.

"Dad, I know you're against long-distance relationships."

"It's not that I'm against them, it's just that I'm speaking from personal experience," he said. He pushed his plate away, the second helping untouched.

"With who?" Leah asked, frowning. "Mom?"

Jim shook his head. "No, with Donna. Brent's mother."

"Mrs. St. James?" Leah asked, incredulous. "I thought you two were just high-school sweethearts. How long did you go out?"

Jim glanced up at the ceiling, thinking. "I don't know. Maybe five years."

"Five years! You made it sound like you just went out a couple of times. What happened?" She rested her elbow on the table and cupped her chin with her hand.

"When I went off to college, we wrote a lot of letters to each other as long-distance phone calls were too expensive. Then I went off to war and it just didn't work out." He was not going to tell his daughter that he had asked Donna to marry him. Some things needed to remain private. "Even the best relationships have difficulty surviving the distance."

"What about 'absence makes the heart grow fonder'?"

"That's crap."

"You would be against me being in a long-distance relationship with Brent?"

Jim shook his head. "No, but I don't want to see you get hurt. You'll be in California living your own life, a life Brent has no idea about. And he'll be here. I just don't see how it could work."

"Well, thanks for your input, Dad," she said sourly.

"Leah, you know me by now. I'm not going to sugarcoat anything. Just giving you some things to think about."

But with the reminder that long-distance relationships didn't work, he came to a conclusion about his own life.

CHAPTER 13

*D*onna had been home from work for an hour when she heard knocking at her side door. She laid down her knitting, muted the Christmas movie she'd been watching, and sighed. There were only a few days left until the festival and she was seriously behind.

She was surprised to see Jim at the side door. When she opened it, he held up a plastic bag and said, "I've got two rib-eye steaks I was planning on grilling tonight, but Leah's not going out and if I want to survive, I can't grill steaks with my vegan daughter in the house."

Donna laughed and opened the door wider. "Come on in."

Once in the kitchen, Jim said, "I hope I'm not interrupting."

Donna shook her head. "Not at all. Actually, I was skipping dinner because I'm so far behind on my yarn-bombing project."

"Then I arrived right in the nick of time. If you don't mind, I'll cook dinner and you go back to knitting."

Donna smiled. She warmed quickly to the thought of a man cooking dinner for her. It was cold out and he was offering to cook a steak for her. It was an offer that was hard to refuse.

"Do you have some salad or something?" Jim asked.

Donna nodded. "Yes, in the crisper. In the pantry, there's a bag of potatoes as well as a box of rice."

"Which do you prefer?" he asked.

Donna thought for a moment. "Surprise me."

"Okay, I will." Jim smiled. "How do you like your steak cooked?"

"Medium," she said. "The grill is out of propane but the broiler will do."

"Great. You sure you don't mind me taking over your kitchen?"

"Not at all," Donna said truthfully.

She sat back down on the sofa in her living room and listened to drawers and cupboard doors opening and closing in her kitchen as Jim searched for things to get dinner ready. It was such an alien sensation—someone cooking a dinner for her in her own kitchen —that she could hardly concentrate on her knitting. She turned off the television deciding she'd much rather listen to Jim puttering around her kitchen, instead.

"Where are your plates, Donna?" Jim called from the kitchen.

"In the drawer underneath the counter," she answered.

She did not say anything when he set up the dining-room table. She noticed he'd even brought a bottle of wine. He uncorked it, let it sit, and returned to the kitchen. He whistled as he worked, and Donna thought that this was something she could get used to.

Donna lost track of the time, making serious progress with her knitting when Jim appeared in the doorway. "Dinner is served."

Smiling, she set her knitting aside. It smelled wonderful and her stomach growled in response.

On the dining-room table were two plates of rib-eye steak, baked potatoes, green beans, and a fresh tossed salad. This was so much better than the ham sandwich she likely would have made for herself.

"It's perfect," Donna announced, looking at it and then looking up at Jim.

He smiled sheepishly, then clapped his hands. "Let's sit down and eat before it gets cold."

Donna tried to ignore her sweaty palms and racing heartbeat. But that was the effect he had on her.

There was a small pat of butter melting and pooling on her steak. She cut a piece and put it into her mouth.

She groaned her approval. "This is absolutely delicious, Jim. Thank you," she said.

He smiled and winked. "My pleasure."

As they ate their meals, Donna was surprised at how hungry she was.

"Have the kids had a falling out?" Jim queried.

"I suppose by 'kids' you mean Brent and Leah," Donna said.

"That's exactly who I mean. For the last two weeks, they've been out every night together and then last night, Leah came home early, and tonight they didn't go out at all," Jim said.

"I haven't spoken to Brent since yesterday," Donna said. "He said Leah was going over to his house and they were baking or something." Donna paused, her fork midair. "But you say Leah returned early?"

Jim nodded and chewed thoughtfully. When finished, he said, "Leah was kind of quiet today. Almost sullen."

"Maybe they had an argument," Donna suggested, worry filling her. Brent had finally found a girl, and it sounded like it was over before it had even begun.

"An argument?" Jim asked. "Already? They've only been seeing each other for a couple of weeks. What could they possibly be fighting about?"

"Who knows?" Donna sighed.

Jim took a sip of his wine. "I should confess that Leah

mentioned she and Brent were considering a long-distance relationship when she returns to California after the holidays."

"Oh."

"I kind of told her my views on that. Based on personal experience."

"Oh, you didn't," Donna said, wincing.

"I did, because I don't want to see either one of them get hurt."

Donna fidgeted with her wine glass. "I understand that our own experience in that department may color your opinion, but they're both grown adults who are capable of making up their own minds."

"Long distance in this age of immediate gratification? Please," Jim countered.

"Does Leah like Brent?" Donna asked.

"Very much so."

This felt encouraging to Donna, but she'd have to find out if Brent felt the same way. If he and Leah had already discussed the possibility of continuing on opposite sides of the country, then he must feel the same way. Brent wasn't an impulsive person. He would have thought this through. And as his mother, she would support his decision, whether she agreed with it or not.

They finished the rest of their meal in thoughtful silence, and then Donna got up to clear the plates. "I got some Christmas cookies yesterday. Will you have some?"

"Yes, please. Leah made some vegan shortbreads, but they're not the same," he said with a grimace.

Donna put on a pot of coffee and laid out a variety of Christmas cookies on a platter. Once she poured the coffee and sat down, she took a frosted cut-out and bit into it. She noticed that Jim had already eaten three cookies. She smiled to herself.

"I hope I haven't put my foot in it," Jim said thoughtfully, reaching for another cookie.

Oh, Jim.

DONNA STOPPED at Brent's house after work the following evening. She hated to ambush him but she needed to get to the bottom of things.

"Mom, what are you doing here?" he asked.

She held up a bag from Bed Bath & Beyond. "There was a sale. I picked up some bedsheets and towels for you."

"Um, okay," he said. He wore a T-shirt and sweatpants. His bare arms made Donna feel cold.

Donna followed him in and set the bag down on the kitchen table, which was set with a lone place setting. She looked around. There was a Christmas tree up in the living room, fully decorated.

"Oh, you got your tree up," she said.

"Leah and I put it up the other night," he said, but he didn't look at it.

He looked at his dinner plate. "Gee, Mom, I didn't know you were coming over. I didn't cook enough."

"I'm not hungry. Sit down and eat your dinner before it gets cold."

She watched him eating his dinner all by himself and her heart ached.

"Why don't you turn on the lights on the tree?" she asked, thinking it would cheer things up.

He didn't lift his head up from his meal. "Nah, I'll do it later."

Donna got a glass out of the cabinet, filled it with water, and sat down.

"Where's Leah tonight?" she asked. "You two seem to be seeing a lot of each other."

"Not anymore. It isn't going to work out," he replied, his voice trailing off.

"Oh no, why not?" Donna asked. She could hear the hurt in her son's voice.

"She's going back to California after Christmas," Brent said. Donna thought he looked a little lost, and she was moved to help him.

"Not ideal, but not impossible," she said.

"More like impossible. I'm tied to Orchard Falls—I can't just uproot and move. I've got too much invested in the clinic."

"That's true."

"And I don't think Leah wants to settle here."

"Have you asked her?"

"No."

Donna wanted to roll her eyes but refrained. *What am I going to do with you?* She wondered.

"Do you like this girl?"

Brent nodded enthusiastically.

Donna sighed in exasperation. "If you like her that much, then tell her how you feel. Ask her to stay."

Brent seemed to consider this for a moment. His jaw clenched and unclenched.

"But she could just stay. She doesn't need me to ask her," Brent said.

Now Donna did roll her eyes. Sometimes Brent was too practical for his own good. "I don't know much about Leah. But if you like this girl, maybe you should sit down with her and find out what she does want. Does she want to leave California?"

"That's ridiculous. She doesn't need my permission to move to Orchard Falls," Brent said.

"Of course not," Donna agreed. "But does she know that you would like her to?"

"No," he said.

"Then ask her. Give her options. If she says no, then you'll know for sure. I don't want to see you spending the rest of your life wondering."

Brent nodded. He finished the last bit of his dinner and said, "Hey, she said something about you and her father dating back in high school."

"That's true, we did," Donna said quietly.

"There was someone before Dad?" he asked incredulously.

Donna nodded. "Yes."

Brent laughed. "It must have been a shock when you discovered he was living right next store."

Donna raised her eyebrows. "Just a bit."

"You're both single. Any chance the two of you might reconnect?" Brent asked.

"Actually, we have decided to take things slow."

Brent's eyes widened. "Really? Wow, Mom, that's great."

"I like him, but he's also entertaining a job offer in California."

"Maybe you could go with him."

"How could I go with him?" Donna asked, looking at her son. "You're here. I couldn't leave you."

"Mom," Brent started with a sigh. "You need to live your own life."

Donna didn't say anything.

"Since Dad died, I don't ever remember you going out on a date. Ever."

Donna shrugged. "After your dad died, I just wasn't interested. Plus, I was happy raising you."

"Mom, I'm raised," he said pointedly. "And I can't thank you enough for the sacrifices you've made. But you're always so worried about me and my personal life when you don't have a personal life of your own." He paused and added, "Maybe it's time to rejoin the land of the living."

Donna smiled at her son. "When did you get so chatty?"

Brent laughed. "Leah must be rubbing off on me." He looked off into the distance. "You know she talked me into performing at the talent show?"

Donna gasped. "She didn't!"

"She did. We're going as Captain and Tennille. She said I'd be perfect as Captain, as he was a man of few words."

"Do you even know who Captain and Tennille were?"

"I do now," he said wryly.

Leah hadn't known her son long, but she already understood him.

Somehow, this had to work out between them.

"Call her," Donna suggested. "Tell her how you feel."

Brent smiled. "I will, Mom."

CHAPTER 14

*I*t was the day before the Snowball Festival was to kick off. Jim had offered to help Donna and her knitting group yarn bomb Main Street, but first he had a quick stop to make at Mr. Brenneman's hardware store to see if the Christmas lights for the community center had arrived. He glanced at his watch and thought he'd better get a move on as he had to pick Donna up in an hour.

There was a small crowd in the hardware store when he entered. He looked around for Mr. Brenneman but didn't see him. The clerk at the till—a young girl—told him he was in his office.

Whistling, Jim headed to the back room and found Mr. Brenneman at his desk with a ledger spread out before him. Mr. Brenneman leaned over it, writing figures neatly into the columns in black pen.

Jim gave a knock on the door.

Mr. Brenneman looked up and smiled. "Jim! Come in."

Jim did so and sat down in a chair next to the desk. "Just checking to see if those lights came in yet."

Mr. Brenneman shook his head. "I'm sorry, Jim. This is a different supplier than the one I usually order from."

Jim stretched his legs. "Don't worry about it."

Mr. Brenneman closed the ledger and set his pen down. "Let's go out and look on the floor and see what we can substitute."

"That's not necessary," Jim said, getting comfortable in the chair.

But Mr. Brenneman was already standing up. "Of course it is! You've got to have lights for the festival."

Jim followed him back out to the store. Once they'd gotten some lights, Jim sat down with his former boss in his office for some conversation and a bottle of cream soda. Forty minutes later, he emerged from the hardware store with a bagful of lights. It was an assortment of interior and exterior lights. And there were only single sets of each kind. But it was all they had, and Jim thought it would have to do.

DONNA WAS JUST STEPPING out of her house when Jim pulled into her driveway. She carried a box in her hands and laid it on a short tower of containers already stacked on the pavement. As they loaded the boxes of knitted items into his car, Jim told Donna about the fact that the Christmas lights had never arrived.

Donna groaned. "No Christmas lights?"

"Mr. Brenneman and I managed to get some lights anyway," he explained. "Now, they're not all the same ones, they're different varieties but you will have lights."

Donna reached out and laid her hand on his arm. "Thanks, Jim, I appreciate your effort. It will be fine."

Once the car was loaded up, they hopped in the front and pulled their seat belts on.

Donna's eyes were clear and bright on the ride over as she chatted about the evening ahead. She stopped talking to look at him. "Are you laughing at me?" she asked, tilting her head.

"Of course not. I'm enjoying your enthusiasm," he said.

Donna's exuberance was tempered when she suddenly thought about Brent. "Brent told me that there was no sense in continuing the relationship with Leah, as the distance is a problem."

Jim sighed. "Leah more or less told me the same thing."

Neither said a word for a moment, but Jim finally spoke. "Why, then, is Leah so miserable?"

Donna shrugged. "I got the same impression from Brent. That he was very disappointed that it didn't work out." Donna paused and looked at Jim. "I told him to call her and sort it out."

"Playing matchmaker?" He grinned.

Donna sighed. "I don't know. Their obstacles are legitimate."

Jim looked over at Donna. "There is no such thing as an insurmountable obstacle. If you can't get over it, you go around it."

Donna raised her eyebrows. "Is this some kind of military lingo?"

"No, it's from the Jim O'Hara belief system."

She couldn't help smiling. "That's worse."

By the time Jim parked behind the library, they had decided not to meddle any further and to let Brent and Leah figure it out themselves.

The members of Donna's knitting group were all assembled inside the library, including Alice. All eyes drifted to Jim when he entered with Donna.

Betty smiled at Jim and asked, "Are you here to help?"

"Yes, ma'm," he said.

"What can you do?" she grilled.

"I've never met a ladder I couldn't climb," he said.

There was a babble of laughter from the group.

It was decided that Alice and another member of the knitting group would remain inside the library while the rest of the members went up and down the street for the yarn bombing. Everyone had their assigned targets.

It turned out that Jim did indeed have a handy skill. Donning his reading glasses, he became the expert at threading yarn through yarn needles so the items could be stitched together around trees and lampposts. As Donna worked on her tree trunks, she watched with amusement as Jim ran up and down Main Street, helping each member of the knitting group with their intended targets. Sometimes it was something as simple as reaching the top of the lamppost rather than always pulling the ladder out. For the trickier, out of reach targets, he walked, with the ladder slung over his shoulder going from one target to the next. He started with the lampposts and ended with Horace. Each time, he took direction from the member of the knitting group before climbing the ladder to affix the knitwear.

When they were finished and the group dispersed, Jim drove Donna home. When he dropped her off, she asked, "Would you like to come over for some hot chocolate?" she asked.

"I'd love to but I can't," he said.

She looked at him expectantly.

"I'm going out at midnight to help with the soup table. I've got to get a quick nap in before I go."

Donna laughed, her eyes crinkling. "I understand. Maybe another time."

"Definitely."

She hesitated, her hand on the door and added, "Would you mind if I went with you later tonight? To the soup table?"

"Not at all," he said. He'd love for her to come along with him and see what it was all about.

"Great. Why don't you come over half an hour before you want to leave and we'll have a cup of hot chocolate?"

"Perfect. See you then."

By THE TIME Jim arrived at Donna's house later that evening, she was pouring hot chocolate into two mugs for them. They sat down next to each other on the sofa. As they did, Jim's thigh brushed up against hers and his heart rate shot up. Christmas music played in the corner on the stereo. Jim thought he could get used to this very easily. And very happily.

After two mugs, Jim saw it was getting late and he knew she had to work in the morning.

"We better get going," he said, standing up.

Donna jumped up from the sofa and took the two empty mugs into the kitchen. After she rinsed out the mugs and set them in the sink.

"Dress warm, the night air can be bitter," he advised.

"Will do," Donna said and she disappeared upstairs.

Jim put on his coat and scarf and waited in the kitchen. His knit cap was in his jacket pocket. Standing at that table for more than an hour by the underpass could leave you very cold. But no colder than those poor souls who slept beneath the underpass. Donna reappeared in the kitchen wearing a heavy sweater over a turtleneck and jeans. She chatted as she put on a hat, scarf, and coat.

He smiled at her.

"What? Is it too much?" she asked.

He shook his head. "No, Donna. It's just perfect." He thought to himself, *You're perfect.*

It was nice to have company as he walked toward the underpass.

Donna mentioned that she was worried about the supposed warm front rolling into the area on Saturday. Jim told her not to worry. That it was still pretty cold. And at least there was still Friday for ice skating and tobogganing. Her excitement was contagious. He knew he loved Donna. And maybe for him the love had always been there. Dormant. He wondered if Donna could ever feel the same way. He chose to be hopeful.

And could he remain her next-door neighbor if she didn't? He knew he couldn't. He was too old for disappointment. And at their age, you either knew or you didn't.

Later, as they walked home, he could see Donna was shivering, and he picked up the pace, wanting to get her back to her warm house.

"Serving those people really puts things in proper perspective for me," Jim said.

"It's amazing how it can do that," Donna said, her teeth chattering.

"It makes me grateful and not wanting to take things for granted," he said.

"Exactly."

"You know that job offer in California?"

Donna nodded. "I do. Have you decided what to do?"

"I'm going to wait one year to see how it goes in Orchard Falls. Who knows, by then the job may not even be available. But Donna, if I go, I'd like to invite you to come to California with me. Now, I know you said you'd never leave here . . ."

"Well, I guess a lot would depend on how this year goes, Jim, but I would give it serious thought." They stopped and faced each other on the sidewalk.

"You would?"

She nodded and smiled. They started walking again toward home.

He couldn't ask more than that from her.

CHAPTER 15

*D*onna couldn't wait to go to work on Friday morning, if only to see the effects of the yarn bombing along Main Street. She left home ten minutes earlier than usual because it had snowed again overnight and she wanted to have time to drive up and down the street.

It looked even better than she'd imagined it would. The whole of Main Street was decked out in brightly colored knitwear. Every tree had a knitted cozy around its trunk. Every pole for a street sign, traffic sign, or lamppost was covered with something knitted. And Horace looked dapper with his new scarf, courtesy of Alice Kempf. It looked great. Excitement filled Donna in anticipation of the upcoming weekend.

Her plan was to leave work early at three so she'd be able to enjoy the ice skating and the toboggan races later that evening. She and Jim were spending the evening and the next day together, either working the festival or partaking in it. For the first time in a long time, Donna was happy. For years she'd been content, but this was something different. And this happiness she felt made her feel younger.

Donna was at the community center late that afternoon when Christine walked in.

"The ice sculptures are here," Christine announced. She waved Donna on. "Come outside and see."

Donna, who had just pulled her coat off, shrugged it back on and followed Christine outside. The weather forecast called for unseasonably warm weather coming in later that night, but Donna had a hard time believing that. At that moment, it was cold and crisp outside and she shivered in her coat.

In front of the community center was a long, refrigerated truck. A young man in his twenties jumped down from the cab.

"Hey, Sam," Christine said, smiling.

"Hey, Mrs. Horst, how are you?" he said. He removed his baseball cap and nodded toward Donna. Christine introduced them.

Sam released the latch at the back of the truck and with a good tug, the back door flew up. Donna's eyes widened and her hands flew to her mouth when she saw the contents of the truck.

"Oh gosh!" Donna exclaimed.

Beaming, Christine looked from the truck back to Donna.

The vehicle was filled with life-sized Christmas ice sculptures. There was a Santa Claus. A reindeer. A snowman, an angel. A Christmas tree. At the back were more sculptures of various holiday themes.

"I can't thank you enough for picking these up for me and transporting them," Christine said to Sam.

"No problem, Mrs. Horst. I'm glad you called," he said.

"Oh, I thought you were the sculptor," Donna said.

"No, he's on the other side of the state." Sam laughed.

Christine laughed. "No, Donna, Sam used to be in one of my Boy Scout troupes. I knew he drove a refrigerated truck, so I gave him a ring and asked him to pick them up."

"Well thank you for transporting them, Sam," Donna said graciously.

"Let's not stand around gawking. Let's get these things out of the back of the truck!" Christine said enthusiastically.

"Where do you want them?" Sam asked Christine.

Donna and Christine looked at each other. Christine asked, "Where do we want them?"

"Oh gee, I hadn't gotten that far," Donna said. How had she missed this? Because she'd assumed Christine would have taken care of it. But truly it had been her responsibility. At the very least, she should have checked with Christine. Quickly, Donna looked around. "I don't know if we can just put them on the sidewalks in front of the shops; we might need a license for that or something," Donna muttered.

"What about in front of the town hall? The square with Horace?" Christine suggested.

"Yes, that's perfect," Donna agreed. There was a large amount of green space around the statue and as it was now covered in snow, it would be perfect.

"Okay, Sam, we need you to drive this down to the other end of Main Street."

Sam nodded, closed up the truck, and jumped back up into the cab. Christine got in on the passenger side. "I can handle this from here, Donna," Christine said.

"I was going to call Walt and make sure we had permission," Donna said, referring to the mayor.

"I'll talk to Walt when I'm there," Christine said.

"That's great," Donna said. It was one less thing for Donna to do. Donna watched the truck pull away, hoping her lack of sorting out a venue for the ice sculptures was the only hitch for the festival.

At six, Jim picked Donna up from the community center to drive out to Snow Ridge Way just outside of town, where there was a toboggan run and ski lifts. She and Jim were helping out with refreshments in the chalet for the toboggan race.

There were about twenty other townspeople volunteering at the event. The mayor would be there soon to open the festival with the races. Jim went to help the crew setting up tables and chairs. Donna joined the team in the kitchen making urns of hot coffee, tea, and cocoa. They arranged paper lace doilies on plastic silver trays and doled out all the donations of Christmas cookies, cakes, and bars.

As Donna laid out a platter of cookies on one of the tables covered in holiday-print paper tablecloths, Sarge reached out for two cookies.

"Don't mind if I do," Sarge said. She was all bundled up for the toboggan races in a blue plaid Elmer Fudd hat and a scarf wrapped several times around her neck.

"All ready for the races?" Donna asked her. The toboggan races were Sarge's favorite event. She'd competed in more races than Donna could count, and she took it very seriously.

"I was up early this morning waxing the bottom of my toboggan," Sarge said, biting into a cookie.

"What does the wax do?" Donna asked.

"Makes the toboggan go faster," Sarge replied.

"Is that allowed in the race rules?" Donna asked.

Sarge shrugged. "I don't know. But I've been waxing my bottom since 1972."

"Oh," Donna said, trying not to laugh.

"I've got to go—don't want to miss the start because I was eating Christmas cookies," Sarge said with almost a smile.

"Good luck," Donna said.

Sarge stopped in her tracks and turned around to face Donna. She was now scowling.

"What did you say?" Sarge asked.

"Good luck?" Donna said, unsure. "Okay, then, break a leg!"

Sarge sighed. "Donna, are you serious? You just jinxed me!"

Before Donna could protest and do something wild like tell Sarge she was overreacting, Sarge stomped off.

The volunteers took a break and stepped outside to watch the start of the races. There were ten toboggan chutes, and all the sleds were in place and ready to go. The mayor stood at the top of the chutes and held a starter pistol up in the air, and as soon as the crack of the report was heard, the toboggans were off, hurtling down the chutes. In the middle chute were Sarge and Ralph and their crew of four other people, most likely their neighbors or customers from the shop. Sarge tended to randomly assign people to her toboggan, and one didn't dare refuse. Donna had been asked once, about twenty years earlier, and was never asked again. These days, Sarge had it down to a science as to the height and weight requirements of the people on her team in order to maximize the speed.

Donna shivered, rubbed her arms, and went inside, not waiting to see who was declared the winner. She and the other volunteers began to set out the carafes of hot beverages, as the tobogganers would be arriving soon, their cheeks flushed and all excited, recounting their runs. What had gone wrong and what had gone right. But the excited, charged crowd never arrived.

Frowning, Donna stopped what she was doing and tilted her head. There was a change in the atmosphere. Instead of the noise of excited racers, the sound was one of frantic voices and yelling and shouting. Quickly, she set down the carafe she was holding and ran to the door along with everyone else. As she did, sirens wailed in the distance.

"Oh no," she whispered, more to herself than to anyone.

When the door was opened and she stepped outside, there was frenetic activity and shouting. People were running away from the lodge, coming down from the chutes, and running to the dense copse of trees beyond the end of the toboggan run. Donna sighed. It had been brought up year after year that the wooded area was going to cause trouble one of these days for a high-speed toboggan. *And that day is today*, Donna thought sadly.

As someone rushed past, coming up from the hill, Donna reached out and asked, "Hey, what's going on?"

It was Stan, who owned the car dealership just outside of town, who replied. "Somebody was hit by a toboggan!"

Donna's hands flew to her mouth. "Oh no!"

"I've got to direct the paramedics!" Stan shouted and ran to meet the ambulance, which was just arriving in the parking lot. The flashing lights and the obnoxious siren disrupted the idyllic winter setting. EMTs jumped out of the ambulance and pulled a gurney out of the back. They navigated the snow with the gurney, looking grim-faced but determined. Donna hoped that whoever it was would be okay.

One of the women standing next to her had walked down the hill a bit to gather information and returned shortly with a look of worry on her face. She said to Donna, "They're saying it's Sarge!"

"Sarge?" Donna repeated, feeling all the color drain from her face.

They all stood there, tense and waiting, the refreshments forgotten. Jim appeared and stood next to Donna.

"Is it Sarge?" Donna asked, searching his face and hoping it wasn't.

"Yeah, she and Ralph and their team came in second place. Sarge gets off the toboggan and starts telling her crew what they did wrong when another toboggan came by and clipped her."

"Is she all right?"

Jim hesitated. "It looked like her leg was broken."

Donna cringed.

"What's wrong? You're as white as a ghost!" Jim said. Usually, she'd find the concern for her on his face very sexy but not at this moment. She recounted her exchange with Sarge before the race.

Jim laughed. "Come on, you did not jinx her. Sarge wouldn't blame you."

Donna raised her eyebrows. "You've apparently forgotten Sarge."

Jim went to say something, but they were distracted by the paramedics wheeling a gurney with Sarge strapped to it. From where she stood, Donna saw the state of Sarge's leg and whispered, "Oh, no."

When Sarge spotted Donna, she sat up, pulling the oxygen mask from her face. She looked straight at Donna and asked, "Happy?"

Donna wanted to crawl down the snow-covered slope and just die in the densely wooded copse.

"Donna, do not blame yourself," Jim said. "These things happen. Unfortunately."

"But Sarge will blame me. I'll have to find a new grocery store," Donna lamented.

Jim laughed. "No, you won't." He reached for her gloved hand and gave it a reassuring squeeze. "Come on, let's go inside and get some coffee."

Donna was grateful for the distraction of Jim. For the rest of the evening, he kept her occupied and she was able to put Sarge's future wrath out of her mind, at least for the time being. She hoped that was the worst that would happen at the weekend's festival.

CHAPTER 16

The following morning, Jim, still half asleep, stepped outside to grab the morning paper and did a double take. He blinked hard to make sure he wasn't imagining things.

All the snow was gone. Every last bit of it. There were patches of grass showing that he hadn't seen since October. Shiny, wet asphalt and mucky lawns were what was left. The meteorologist had said a warm front was moving through the area, but when were they ever right? He straightened up and drew in a deep breath. The air was practically balmy for December.

He headed back inside and put on the coffee. Hazel walked slowly into the kitchen, regarded Jim with curiosity, and meowed. Who knew where Tiny was—probably in the bathroom, using the toilet. If he ever caught that cat taking a newspaper into the bathroom, Jim would move to another state. Hazel had recovered but seemed more fragile than before. She wound herself around Jim's legs and purred loudly.

"Is Leah still sleeping?" he asked the cat. He maneuvered around her carefully, not wanting to accidentally step on her. She'd been through enough. But the cat followed him, rubbing up against his legs and purring.

Sighing, Jim picked up the cat carefully and cradled it. He scratched under her chin and the cat purred louder.

Once Hazel was fed, he poured coffee and sat down. He'd only taken one sip of his coffee when there was a knock at the side door. He glanced at the clock, wondering who was out so early on a Saturday morning.

Donna stood in his driveway with her arms folded against her chest.

"Oh, good, you're up. I was just going to take a ride to see what's left of the ice sculptures," Donna said. But her expression said she knew what condition she'd find them in. "Want to go with me?"

"Let me get my coat" he said. "Do you want me to drive?"

Donna shook her head. "My car is warmed up and ready to go."

After he downed his coffee in one gulp, he grabbed his coat and bundled into it.

As they drove up to Main Street, Jim took in the sight of Donna next to him in the front seat. Her hair shone in the morning sunlight and her eyes were as beautiful and bright as a pair of emeralds. Her face was naked of makeup but she wore perfume, something light and reminding him of vanilla. The thought of how he would like to wake up next to her every morning filled his head.

Saturday-morning traffic was light as they drove along Main Street.

Jim remarked to Donna, "The yarn bombing looks great!"

Donna looked absentmindedly out the window. "Oh yeah."

"Come on, Donna, it's not your fault," Jim said. "No one could have predicted fifty-degree weather in December."

"The National Weather Service predicted it," she said forlornly.

"But they get it wrong more than half the time," he pointed out.

"I suppose," she said. "I should have been more prepared."

"It's not going smoothly, is it?" Jim asked with a sympathetic glance.

"Nothing is ever perfect, I guess," she admitted.

"Nope," Jim agreed. "But it doesn't have to be perfect to be good."

Donna smiled at him.

As they pulled up in front of the town hall, Donna found a spot right out front and parked the car. They stared at the space circling the statue of the town's founder that had previously been occupied by ice sculptures just yesterday afternoon. It was all gone. There wasn't even an indistinguishable pile of slush to give testimony that they'd been there in the first place.

"I don't believe this," Donna groaned. "I'll have to tell Christine."

Jim leaned over and took her hand in his. "I know you're upset, but there's nothing that can be done about it now. Let me take you to breakfast."

"Okay," Donna said half-heartedly.

They pulled into the parking lot behind the diner and walked around to the front of the building on the sidewalk. Jim held the door for Donna as they entered the restaurant.

Once inside, they were seated by the host, who handed them a menu each. They both said yes to her inquiry of coffee.

The diner was all decked out in Christmas decorations. Gold and silver garland hung from the ceiling with red and green ornaments suspended from the garland. The windows were covered in fake snow, and Christmas lights of red, blue, and green lined the windows. Holiday music floated out from speakers in the corner of the ceiling. Some of the servers wore Santa Claus hats. One server wore candy-cane earrings.

That was one of the things Jim loved about Orchard Falls. The town still went all out for the holidays. Any holiday. Community spirit and involvement made it festive.

Their coffees were brought out and their orders taken.

Steve arrived at their booth to say hello.

"Any word on Sarge?" Donna asked.

"Just that she went in for surgery last night. Broke her leg in two places!" Steve said excitedly.

Donna slumped in the seat and groaned again. "She's going to kill me!"

Steve frowned in confusion. "Why?"

"Because Donna wished her good luck and told her to break a leg before the race," Jim explained.

Steve laughed. "Boy, you live dangerously!"

Steve glanced back and forth between Jim and Donna. "Well, I've got to go. Got to get the boys to their hockey practice. See you both later at either the craft fair or the talent show."

CHAPTER 17

*D*onna threw in a load of wash, then jumped into her car and headed over to Christine's. Her friend lived in an old farmhouse at the other end of Main Street, about six blocks from Donna's house.

As usual, Christine's was a madhouse of activity.

"Mom! Where's my hockey stick?" yelled one of her sons from upstairs.

"Where did you leave it?" Christine shouted. She stood at her kitchen table, folding and sorting laundry from a basket perched on a kitchen chair. There were two more baskets of clean laundry at her feet. The table was covered in piles of folded laundry. She had six sons and two had just arrived home from college for the holidays.

Donna took the basket of towels and began folding, joining her friend at the table.

"Mom!" yelled the same kid again.

"Check the garage and hurry up," Christine said. "Your father will be back soon and he's not coming in, so you better be at the curb."

Donna laughed. "Where's Eugene?"

"It's oil-change day for both cars," Christine explained. "He should be back with my car soon and he has to drop the boys off to hockey practice."

As if on cue, a car horn blared from outside.

"Matt! Luke! Dad's outside waiting," Christine called.

Two teenage boys bounded down the stairs sounding like they weighed more than they did, and sailed through the kitchen at a high rate of speed, loaded down with all kinds of hockey gear and equipment.

"Hi, Donna! Bye, Mom," they called as they ran out the door.

Once quiet descended, Christine asked, "How about some coffee?"

Donna shook her head. She was still full from breakfast, where she'd devoured a three-egg omelet, toast, hash browns and two cups of coffee. The stress of the festival was giving her an appetite.

From upstairs, there were repeated thumps and thuds, to the point where the brass lighting fixture directly over the kitchen table began to sway. A small shower of dust fell from the spackled ceiling and landed over the piles of clean laundry.

"Give me strength," Christine muttered. She walked to the foot of the staircase and yelled, "Kevin! Knock it off!"

She headed back to the table. "He's going through either a karate or kung fu phase. Hopefully, it will end soon."

For as long as Donna had known Christine, her life had been chaotic—even before she'd had six sons. Brent used to love going over to their house as a child because it was pure bedlam.

"The ice sculptures are gone."

Christine stopped folding a T-shirt. "Gone?"

"Yeah, as in melted."

Christine peered out the window. "Oh, gosh."

"I'm so sorry, Christine, they were so beautiful."

Christine shrugged. "What are you going to do?"

"I'll have to call the artist and tell him that all his hard work melted," Donna said, not treasuring that idea.

"I'll do it. He should hear it from me." Christine paused and looked up at the ceiling. "Though when I mentioned to him about a possible warm front, he said they'd be fine. 'It won't get that warm,' he said."

"Sarge broke her leg last night at the toboggan races," Donna reported.

Christine had a sly grin on her face. "Too bad it couldn't have been her tongue."

Donna burst out laughing. "Christine!"

"Anyway, where have you been?" Christine asked. "It's like you fell off the face of the earth."

"I've been busy with this festival. Hopefully, nothing else will go wrong," Donna said.

They looked at one another and laughed.

"Just the festival?" Christine enquired with one eyebrow raised. "Sure you haven't been busy with your new neighbor slash former boyfriend?"

Donna blushed.

"I knew it!" Christine said. She pushed the laundry aside and sat down across from Donna. "Tell me."

Donna shrugged. "There's not much to tell. We've been hanging out."

"Hanging out?" Christine scowled. "That's what my boys do. At least tell me you guys have kissed?"

"Well, no," Donna said and added quickly, "Not yet."

Christine shook her head. "What's wrong? You like him and he likes you. So why aren't you kissing each other?"

"Oh Christine," Donna said, squirming in her seat.

"Don't 'oh Christine' me," she shot back with a smirk.

"We're taking it slow," Donna said.

Christine made a face. "How slow is slow? Do you think you'll be kissing by next year?"

Donna owed Jim a kiss. He'd said so himself. Her stomach fluttered at the thought of it. She didn't think he'd wait until next year to collect it. And she didn't want to wait. Donna wanted Jim to kiss her. More than anything.

"We want to proceed with caution."

Christine rolled her eyes. "What are you? A school bus moving on after the red light changes?"

Donna started laughing. "We just want to take our time. Enjoy the journey."

Christine scowled. "That's crap. Live your life. Kiss the man. Kiss him now."

"I don't know if this is a long-term relationship. He's considering a job in California."

"So? Go with him. Live your life," Christine said in exasperation.

"And . . ."

"And what?"

"I'm spooked."

Christine frowned. "About what?"

"Jim and I were already together once, and it didn't work out."

"Second chances anyone?" Christine was always ready with an answer, and it was usually the right one.

"Plus, there's the whole thing about Brad."

"What about Brad?"

"You remember when I first started dating Brad, how I told you he was the perfect rebound relationship because he was so different than Jim?"

Christine nodded. They'd spent many a night talking about this, either in Donna's bedroom or Christine's bedroom with the

CDs playing in the background. At the time, Christine had already gotten engaged to Eugene.

"It was a very unexpected happiness I found with Brad," Donna admitted.

Christine agreed and said quietly, "Brad was a beautiful man."

"I mean, no one was more surprised than me that it worked out the way it did between us."

"Honey, the two of you were perfect together."

"It didn't work out the first time with Jim. Who's to say it will work out a second time? Am I being greedy for wanting another chance at happiness when I already had it once? Jim is not Brad."

Christine lowered her voice. "No, he isn't. He's Jim. I don't believe in all this superstitious nonsense. I believe in living your life to the fullest. And as soon as all my kids are gone off to college, that's what I plan on doing. Actually, I may move to another state altogether and not leave Eugene or the boys my forwarding address."

They both laughed.

"But seriously. May I point out a few things?"

"Please do."

"First, Brad loved you madly and he'd want you to be happy. I know that's a cliché, but it's true. And if you think you have a chance of happiness with Jim, then take it."

Donna hesitated.

Christine continued. "Second, Jim is not Brad. They're at opposite ends of the spectrum. But you're also not the same person you were thirty years ago or even twenty years ago. None of us are." She paused. "What I'm saying is, Jim and Brad— apples and oranges. We like them both but for different reasons."

"You've certainly been a good sounding board, Christine." Donna smiled.

"That's what best friends are for. Really, though, Donna, be happy. Not content. Happy." Christine appeared thoughtful as she picked up the last item of clothing from the basket. "And who's to say you can't love more than one person during your lifetime?"

THE COMMUNITY CENTER was packed for the talent show.

Donna scanned the room. It was packed. Along the walls were the winter wonderland decorations the art department from the high school had created. There were intricate, glittery snowflakes of all different sizes suspended from the ceiling and along the walls were murals of snow-capped mountains and chalets. They'd done a gorgeous job.

The center's lights were dimmed except for the mishmash of Christmas lights strung along the perimeter of the ceiling and around the inside of the windows. Some were multicolored, some were clear, some were blue, some blinked and some didn't. Donna tried to look on the bright side and thought that at least they had lights. Donna remembered Jim's words that it didn't have to be perfect to be good. She just hoped it didn't turn into an epic failure. She didn't want to think about what else could go wrong.

Brent stepped out from behind the heavy red drapes and up to the mic and into the spotlight to begin his emcee duties.

Donna could tell he was nervous by the way he stumbled over some words and his rapid-pitch delivery. She sat on a folding chair next to Jim in the sixth row. Jim reached over and squeezed her thigh. Donna's breath caught in her throat at his touch.

"There has been . . . um . . . one change in tonight's program. Sarge and Ralph will not be performing their duet of "Islands in the Stream" tonight due to an unforeseen circumstance." This was met by "aws" from the audience. "Instead, Alice Kempf has graciously agreed to step in and conduct a Christmas sing-along with the audience as she plays the piano." There was subdued clapping for that.

Donna nodded her approval. What was a talent show without music? A sing-along was sure to put everyone in the spirit. And kudos to Alice for agreeing to be a last-minute replacement. She sighed. Orchard Falls was a great little town. She wished Jim could see it the way she did.

Later, after Alice stood up from her piano bench, the crowd jumped to its feet to give their oldest resident a standing ovation.

When Brent and Leah appeared for their act, Donna and Jim sat up straighter in their seats. Jim leaned into Donna. "This could be the start of something big." In the hushed dark, with his shoulder touching hers, Donna's skin tingled.

Brent and Leah were dressed like Captain and Tennille. Brent sported a navy-blue nautical jacket, hat, and white pants. Leah wore a blonde pageboy wig. As Brent began to play the piano poorly, Leah sang off-key.

Brent could not take his eyes off Leah. Donna put her hand to her mouth as she saw first- hand that her son was absolutely smitten with Jim's daughter.

When they were finished, Jim whispered, "Hollywood has nothing to worry about."

Donna elbowed him with a giggle.

Jim sighed. "They've got it bad for each other, don't they?"

Donna smiled. "They sure do."

CHAPTER 18

*J*im hesitated in the doorway of his kitchen. Leah stood at the table, wrapping Christmas presents.

"It's okay, Dad, you can come in. I've already wrapped your gift," she said, waving the tape dispenser around.

Every kitchen chair was occupied by shopping bags or tubes of wrapping paper. Leftover scraps of paper and ribbon and empty wrapping-paper tubes littered the floor.

"So, no coal for me this year," Jim joked.

"Nope." She smiled. "You've been good."

"Something smells good," Jim said, looking over to the pot on the stove.

"I'm making potato-and-leek soup for tomorrow," she said.

Jim clapped his hands. "Sounds good."

"Where are you going?" she asked, cutting a sheet of wrapping paper to fit the box she'd laid on top of it.

"Over to the community center to help get ready for the dance tonight," he replied.

"Geez, you've really settled in to Orchard Falls," she said.

"I'm getting there. I did grow up here, you know," he said.

"I've fallen in love with it," she said. "It's a lovely little town."

Jim raised his eyebrows and grinned. "Does this have anything to do with the town's veterinarian?"

Leah blushed. "Oh, Dad." She set the scissors down. "Actually, I was thinking of staying on after Christmas."

"Really?" Jim asked, not overly surprised.

"Would that be all right?"

"Of course, it's all right with me. As I've said before, this is your home, too," he said. "You really like Brent."

She nodded and smiled. "We had a long talk and I've decided to stay a little while longer."

"It sounds like you didn't have to think about it too much."

"No."

"What about your job? And the activism?" he asked.

"I can be an activist anywhere. And I've already talked to my boss and I'm going to put in for a transfer to the east coast. They were planning on opening another branch out here for guide-dog trainers, and I told them Orchard Falls would be perfect as it's only a two-hour drive to New York City."

Jim was delighted that his daughter would be living with him on a more permanent basis. He was even happy that the cats were staying. After all, it was a package deal.

It made Jim happy that his daughter was happy.

THE COMMUNITY CENTER was a picture of organized chaos as volunteers hurried to get everything ready for the dance later that evening. The atmosphere was charged with excitement, and voices laughed loudly. Someone had brought a Bluetooth speaker, and Christmas music filled the center.

The DJ was in the corner, setting up his equipment, and the

caterers were setting up the buffet tables with warming dishes. They asked Donna if she wanted the napkins folded a certain way, but she left it up to them. Donna walked over to the DJ to reiterate that they didn't want the music played so loud that they couldn't carry on a conversation. Jim joined the rest of the volunteers in setting up tables and chairs. The caterers followed immediately behind them, laying tablecloths and place settings and setting down centerpieces.

Ralph arrived with a large light-up snowball that was going to hang over the dance floor. As soon as he appeared, he was swarmed by well-wishers and townspeople enquiring about Sarge.

Jim and Donna joined the small circle.

"How's Sarge doing?" Jim asked.

"She's coming along. She'll have that cast on for a while. She's home, so that's good."

"Is she up for company?" Donna asked. Jim could hear the hope in her voice.

Ralph hesitated. "Give it a few days, Donna."

"So, she blames me," Donna said.

Ralph laughed. "You know Sarge!"

That caused a twitter among the crowd.

"Can I hang that snow globe up for you?" Jim asked.

"No, thanks, Jim. I've got it," Ralph said.

"Let me grab the ladder for you, Ralph," he said.

As Jim headed off to the storage room, the DJ performed a sound check. "*Testing one, two, three, testing one, two, three.*"

Donna made a beeline for the DJ. "That's way too loud!"

After Jim set up the ladder for Ralph, he glanced around the room to make sure all the tables were set up. Then he sought out Donna.

She rubbed the back of her neck and looked around the center. Her gaze bounced from Ralph up on the ladder to the DJ to the caterers and back again to Ralph. She bit her lip as she watched him.

Jim reached out and touched her arm. "Hey, are you all right?" he asked.

"I am," she said, nodding her head so fast that Jim was afraid it was going to pop off.

"Everything is fine," he said.

At that moment, Mary Ellen Schumacher walked in, her hand still in a cast.

Donna groaned. "Is she coming to check up on me? Probably heard about all the various disasters and figures she'd better take it back over before I run the festival right into the ground."

Jim burst out laughing. "I hardly think she's going to sack you. Stop worrying. There's nothing more you can do at this point, so you should go home or you'll end up too exhausted to enjoy yourself tonight. I don't know about you, but I'm looking forward to the fireworks."

Donna grimaced. "There won't be any fireworks tonight. The warm weather last night melted all that snow and flooded the basement where they were being stored."

She looked stressed. And her eyes looked wet. Jim did the only thing he could think of. He took her in his arms and he didn't care who saw it. He pulled her into a tight embrace and whispered in her ear, "Everything is going to be all right. Just take a deep breath for me."

He had no intention of letting her go, but they were interrupted by Mary Ellen.

"Oh, now this is interesting," Mary Ellen said.

Jim and Donna pulled apart and Donna smiled.

"How are things going? Everything looks wonderful!" Mary Ellen enthused.

"Well, we've had a few hiccoughs," Donna admitted.

Mary Ellen smiled but she looked confused. "Such as?"

"Sarge broke her leg, the lights never came in for the hall, the ice sculptures melted, all the snow melted so all outdoor activities had to be canceled today, and now there'll be no fireworks because they were flood damaged."

Mary Ellen seemed unfazed. "That's all?"

Donna's eyes widened.

"The first year I took over, it was like the gates of Hell had opened." Mary Ellen laughed. "Don't you remember, Donna?"

Donna shook her head.

"Let me refresh your memory," Mary Ellen said. She held up her hand and ticked off things on her fingers. "Let's see, the caterer somehow didn't remember to pencil us in, so we had no food for the dinner. We turned it into a potluck where everyone brought a dish, and it was just as nice. There were other things, too; it seemed like everything that could go wrong did go wrong. But the clincher was when the old community center burnt to the ground. Problem with the electrical. Yeah, that was really special," Mary Ellen said. "And yet they asked me to run the festival the year after that."

"Oh, I remember that!" Donna said. "That was your first year? And you were brave enough to take it on the second year?"

Mary Ellen shrugged. "I figured it had been so awful that it could only get better. There are always some problems. Some are big and some are small. But we tend to carry on." She paused and eyed Donna. "But don't let it get to you so much that you can't enjoy yourself. Because then you'll miss the point. As long as everyone has a good time, then it's considered a successful festival."

Donna sighed.

Jim interrupted. "I think you've done enough here, Donna. Go home and do something relaxing."

"Jim's right, Donna, you can only do so much," Mary Ellen

said. "And everyone has said you've done a great job. Go home and we'll see you back here tonight."

Reluctantly, Donna agreed. Jim walked her to her car and made sure she got into it. "Now straight home. Take a nice hot bath, light some candles, relax. I'll pick you up tonight."

"Are you sure?" she asked.

He nodded. "Yeah. You're going to enjoy tonight. All you'll have to do is show up."

WHEN JIM WALKED over to Donna's house later that night, he was stunned into speechlessness at the sight of her. In a green dress that matched her eyes and hugged her figure, she took his breath away. He swallowed hard at the sight of her, and his mouth went dry. He couldn't remember the last time a woman had this kind of effect on him.

She did not break eye contact, her eyes locking on his. He felt like he was melting under her gaze. He ran his finger underneath his collar, trying to loosen it.

He finally managed to say, "Donna, you look stunning."

She smiled, and he held her coat for her and escorted her out the door. He opened the passenger-side door for her and waited until she was settled in her seat before shutting the door. He felt like a teenager on a first date, as he was experiencing the same exact sensations: sweaty palms, racing heartbeat, and a hyper sense of awareness.

By the time Jim walked around to his side of the car, the only thing he knew was that he was going to kiss Donna that night. It felt inevitable.

When he buckled his seat belt, he didn't turn on the car right away. He looked at her in the evening light and said, "I'm a little nervous tonight."

Donna's expression softened and she reached over and gave his hand a gentle squeeze. "I am, too," she admitted.

He brought her hand to his lips and kissed the inside of her wrist.

"Let's do this," he said.

DONNA AND JIM sat at a table near the dance floor with Brent and Leah. The catered dinner was good, and Jim couldn't remember a time when he'd been as happy. After dinner, Brent and Leah excused themselves and said they were stepping outside for some fresh air.

When the music started, he asked Donna to dance—it was as good an excuse as any to take her in his arms. Jim led the way, taking her hand in his. His heart thumped against his chest wall. When he found a spot, he turned and wrapped his arms around her, something he'd been longing to do. He closed his eyes and inhaled. Her perfume was nice, something light and not too overpowering.

Jim closed his eyes briefly and just lived in the moment. As soft music played, he waltzed Donna around the dance floor. It amused him that Donna was the first girl he'd ever danced properly with and he hoped she'd be the last. There was no one else for him but Donna.

Donna tilted her head to look up at him.

He pulled her a little tighter and whispered, "You owe me something."

She smiled, her lips parting slightly. "I know I do."

Fueled by impatience, he couldn't resist, and he leaned in to kiss her. Something he'd thought of doing since that day back in October when she came storming over to his house about that tree in her backyard.

But he was distracted by a strange noise. It sounded like a ripping noise. Jim frowned and looked around.

"What's the matter?" Donna asked.

He narrowed his eyes and listened harder. He looked up just in time to see the big illuminated Christmas snowball loosening from its moorings.

There was a loud crack and Jim had just enough time to say, "Look out!" and grab Donna by her forearms, pushing her out of harm's way.

The giant snowball came down and clipped his forehead as it crashed to the floor. Jim grimaced, falling forward to his knees and landing hard on all fours. Immediately, a gush of blood sprang from the wound. Everybody jumped back and either gasped or screamed. The music stopped and everyone on the dance floor circled the crashed snowball, its lights still twinkling. Donna rushed over to him.

"Jim, you're hurt," Donna said. She put her arms around his shoulders and helped him up.

"I'm okay, it's just a graze," he said, trying to reassure her, but he could feel the blood running down his head to his neck and underneath his collar. "Are you all right?"

Someone handed Donna a stack of napkins from the nearest table, and she applied pressure to the wound on his head. "I'm fine, but you're going to need stitches," she said.

"I don't think so," he said, downplaying it.

"No, I'm taking you to the ER," she said firmly. "No arguments."

"All right." Her tone, indicating that she wouldn't take no for an answer, made Jim feel cared for. Looked after. And he'd been alone for so long, it was a new sensation. One he could easily get used to.

One of the committee members ran over to them with a first aid kit. Donna made Jim sit in a chair so she could take a better look at the wound. He saw her eyes widen at the sight of it when she pulled the napkin away.

Ray Malinowski, the fire chief, applied gauze and a bandage to it until Jim could get to a hospital.

As Donna applied pressure to his gauze, she looked at the debris covering the dance floor and then her gaze shifted back to Jim's head wound. She smirked. "Why am I not surprised?"

And with that, Jim burst out laughing.

CHAPTER 19

*D*onna drove Jim to the emergency room in his SUV while Brent and Leah followed in Brent's car. By the time they arrived, the blood from Jim's head wound had already saturated the bandage and was seeping out around it. The collar of his white shirt was soaked in red.

Donna's knuckles were white on the steering wheel, and her lips pinched together in a thin line.

"Don't worry," Jim assured her. "I'm fine; it doesn't even hurt."

She looked at him in disbelief, cocking an eyebrow.

"Head wounds always bleed profusely," he added.

They argued briefly about Donna dropping Jim off at the front door. He insisted that he was perfectly able to walk from the parking garage, but Donna wouldn't hear of it. She dropped him off at the door of the emergency room and went and parked the car.

When she arrived in the waiting room, Brent and Leah were already there, sitting on the hard, orange plastic chairs. Jim sat at a little cubicle, registering. As Donna sat down next to Brent, she saw Jim pull out his insurance card from his wallet and hand it to the registrar. After ten minutes, he joined them.

After thirty minutes, Brent stood up and asked if anyone wanted coffee.

"There's a donut shop in the lobby," he said.

Donna and Jim declined. Leah looked up at Brent. "I'd love a coffee." They regarded each other with tenderness, as if Donna and Jim weren't there.

"The usual?" Brent asked Leah.

She nodded. "And maybe a donut?" she asked, squinting her eyes as if she was unsure.

"The ones with sprinkles?" he asked, his eyes never leaving her face.

"Yes." She smiled, enthused.

Jim looked at Donna and winked.

After Brent left, the doors to the emergency room opened and a nurse called out Jim's name. Leah accompanied him as his next of kin. Briefly, Donna thought that if she had married Jim, it would be her going back there with him. She wanted to be with him but it wasn't her place.

As Donna sat there alone, waiting, the one thing she kept playing over and over in her head was the fact that when that big snowball fell from the ceiling, Jim, without thinking, had pushed her out of harm's way. She didn't even know how to put into words how much that meant to her. Certainly, with the passage of almost three decades, they had changed as people. She knew she had; life and experience had tempered her youthful enthusiasm. But the passage of time had not erased the connection they shared or the feelings she'd had for him. Still had for him. They may have lain dormant all these years, smoldering, but now they blazed.

Brent returned, carrying two take-out coffee cups and a small paper bag. He nodded toward the emergency-room door. "Has he gone in?"

"Yes."

Brent sat down next to Donna and set the coffees and bagged donut on the small table in front of them, pushing some magazines aside.

"How's it going with you and Leah?" she asked.

Brent smiled. "Good. We had a long talk."

"And? Are you able to tell your mother anything?" she asked with an encouraging smile.

Brent looked so handsome. He seemed more relaxed. Happier. If that was because of Leah, then Donna was all for it. She hoped they would be able to work things out.

"Leah is going to stay in Orchard Falls for the time being," Brent said. "I took your advice and asked her to stay, and she said she would." Brent could barely suppress his smile. Donna was practically moved to tears.

"That's wonderful," she said. "Jim will be delighted."

Brent laughed. "He's not the only one. I really like her, Mom. We have a lot of the same interests and mutual goals," he said.

"I'm happy for you, Brent. You deserve this," Donna said truthfully.

"We'll see how it goes. If all goes well, I'm hoping Leah will become a permanent resident of Orchard Falls."

"Very good," Donna said, happy that her only child may have finally found some personal happiness.

"What about you and Jim?" Brent queried.

Donna shrugged. "It's going fine. We're just enjoying each other's company." She couldn't give him an answer, because she didn't know what the future held for her and Jim. But she had been giving their future some thought and it had resulted in her penning a letter to Jim which she had hoped to give to him after the dance. It remained safely tucked in her purse. She was just waiting for the right time to give it to him.

Leah emerged from the emergency room and said, "They've stitched him up, and they've done a CT scan just to make sure."

Donna nodded. "Good."

Leah looked at Donna and smiled. "He wants to see you."

Donna was pleased he'd asked for her. "All right."

"He's in examination room six."

Donna nodded and headed toward the emergency-room area. Someone was just exiting through the locked doors, and Donna slipped through as unobtrusively as possible.

The emergency room was chaotic. The few times in her life she'd been there, it had always been like this. There were people, doctors, nurses, and other hospital staff moving about in a hurried manner from room to room and around the nurses' station. There was a cacophony of noises: rushed, hurried voices, non-stop ringing of a phone at the nurses' desk, and the constant beeping of monitors.

Donna hesitated in the doorway of room number six. Jim was unaware of her presence. She observed him for a moment. The railroad track of sutures at the top of his forehead. He was sure to be left with a scar, which would only add to his attractiveness, she guessed. His black tuxedo jacket lay on the chair. His white shirt, discarded on the gurney next to him, was crumpled and saturated with blood. It looked beyond salvaging. But it was only a shirt, Donna reminded herself. Easily replaceable. He sat there in his dress pants and a white T-shirt. Her breath caught in her throat.

Donna tapped softly on the doorframe.

He looked up and broke into a smile.

"Donna."

Donna stood next to him and laid her hand on his arm. "How are you?" The room was small but filled with medical paraphernalia. There was a sharps container on the wall and medical waste bins on the floor. There was a small sink with a container of paper towels for drying hands. An assortment of gloves labeled S, M, and L sat in an acrylic holder on the wall.

"I'm fine. Just a bit banged up, that's all," he said with a grin.

"How's your head?" Donna asked with a grimace.

"Fine. They gave me some Tylenol for my headache," Jim said. "Just waiting to get the scan results and then hopefully, I can go home."

"Good."

Jim looked at her. "The night didn't go as planned, did it?"

Donna laughed. "No, it certainly didn't."

"I'm sorry, Donna," Jim said quietly. "I'm sorry for everything."

A lump formed in Donna's throat. She reached for his hand and held it in hers. He looked at her, surprised. "I'm sorry too, Jim."

Donna was about to say something but was interrupted by a third person entering the room. Reluctantly, she let go of Jim's hand and looked at the doctor.

"Mr. O'Hara, I've got the results of your CT scan," the doctor said, his voice booming. He stopped and looked at Donna.

"It's okay, doc," Jim said. He glanced at Donna and smiled. "There are no secrets between us."

"Great," the doctor said. "Your scan was normal. No concussion. The nurse will be in with the discharge paperwork and you'll be free to go. Remember to not get the sutures wet, and follow up with your own doctor to have them removed."

Jim thanked him when he left. Donna leaned against the gurney next to Jim, her arm brushing up against his thigh. She just felt the need to be near him. They waited half an hour before a nurse came with discharge papers.

When they left and headed toward the waiting room, they

found Leah with her head on Brent's shoulder. Donna smiled at the sight. Brent and Leah stood up.

"Ready to go home?" Donna asked.

"I am," Jim said. To Leah, he said, "Honey, it's still early enough for you and Brent to go out. Donna can drive me home." He looked at Donna sheepishly. "You don't mind, do you?"

Donna smiled and shook her head. "No, of course not."

"Are you sure, Dad? I mean, it's almost eleven," Leah said.

Jim nodded. "Eleven—isn't that when you usually go out?"

"Dad," Leah said in a mock scold. She looked to Brent. "Is it too late?"

Brent shook his head and helped Leah into her coat. "No, it's never too late, Leah."

Brent and Leah left, hand in hand. Leah looked back once at her father, who waved her on with a smile. Donna and Jim stood there for a moment, watching the younger couple depart.

Donna insisted Jim wait while she retrieved his car from the parking garage.

When she pulled around to the emergency-room entrance, Jim got into the passenger's side and buckled his seat belt.

Donna wheeled the car around the circle and pulled out onto the main road.

Jim chuckled. "I'm not used to sitting in the passenger seat."

"I bet." She laughed. "Could you get used to it?"

With a grin, Jim answered, "Depends on who the driver is." He lifted an eyebrow.

"What if it were me?" she asked.

Without hesitation, Jim said, "I could definitely get used to that."

Donna felt the heat rise from her chest, creep up her neck, and fan out over her face, and she was pretty sure it wasn't a hot flash.

The drive home, though short, was quiet. When Donna pulled

into Jim's driveway, she asked, "Will I park it in the garage for you?"

"Nah, there's no snow forecasted for tonight," he said.

"I hope we get a white Christmas," Donna said.

Jim's eyes twinkled in the shadowy interior of the car. "If that's what you want, then that's what I want, too," he said.

Neither one of them made a move to get out of the car.

Donna opened her purse and pulled an envelope out.

"Jim, it's been awhile since I've been in a serious relationship," she said. Her voice shook as she spoke. "There are things I want to tell you. I wrote you a letter." She handed him the envelope.

To lighten up the silence that followed, she added, "I thought it best if I hand-delivered it."

Jim let out a bark of laughter. "Donna, you're the absolute best!"

He leaned over to her. "There's a lot I need to say to you, as well."

She laid a finger on his lips. "Shh. Leave it now, until tomorrow." She laughed. "So much has happened tonight."

"Hey, the Snowball Festival is over," Jim said, looking at the clock on the dashboard.

"Thank God." Donna said, then yawned, the events of the past few days catching up with her.

"You're tired. Go inside, and go to bed," Jim said softly.

"Would you like to come over for breakfast tomorrow morning?" she asked. She didn't know why, but she felt shy.

"Don't you have to work in the morning?" he asked.

"No, I took off this week because of Christmas," Donna said.

"Then I'd love to," Jim said. A slow smile spread across his face. "It's a date, then."

Donna smiled, her heart filling up with hope. "I guess it is."

Jim hesitated before getting out. "You know, I planned to kiss you tonight."

She smiled and lifted an eyebrow, secretly pleased.

"But it didn't work out."

"It will," she said softly.

"I want it to be special," he said.

"It will be," she said. It took a Herculean effort not to give in to the impulse to reach for him and pull him into her embrace. Instead, she reached for his hand, squeezed it, and said good night.

CHAPTER 20

$\mathcal{T}$he following morning, Jim examined his sutures in the bathroom mirror, decided he'd definitely seen worse, and brushed his teeth and went about getting dressed. The door to Leah's room was closed. He hadn't heard her come in during the night, but he was pretty sure it had been late.

Before he headed over to Donna's house, he reread her letter. Again. Although it wasn't necessary, as he had it memorized. He hadn't slept well. He'd lain awake thinking of what Donna had written:

Dear Jim,
Since you've come back into my life, you've turned it upside down in ways I would have never dreamed of. But in a good way. I've been alone now for so long that it never occurred to me that I might find love again.
For as long as you've known me, you've known that I've never wanted to leave Orchard Falls. This is my home. It's as much a part of me as I am of it.

There is only one reason I would ever leave, and that reason is love.

You asked me if I would consider going to California with you. My answer is yes.

If you asked me to go to the North Pole, I would say yes. If you asked me to go to the moon with you, I would say yes. And I would be happy about it.

I've always thought of Orchard Falls as my home. But the truth is, my home's where my heart is, and my heart will be wherever you are.

My answer is yes. Yes to you, yes to us. A thousand times yes.

Love,

Donna

DONNA HAD TOLD him to come over at nine. And to bring his appetite. He stepped outside, pulling the door closed behind him and locking it. He glanced up at the gray sky, looking for any signs of snow. He hoped Donna got her white Christmas. Hands in his pockets, he whistled as he cut across the lawn to Donna's house. Anticipation had left him excited and oddly, content.

Donna appeared at the door with a spatula in her hand, wearing an apron decorated in holly and ivy over her clothes. Something smelled good. He could hear Christmas music coming from the living room.

"Jim, there's no need to knock," Donna said.

He smiled, following her into the kitchen. Every burner on the stove was occupied by a pot or a pan.

"Can I ask what's for breakfast?"

"Blueberry pancakes and scrambled eggs," she said. "Bacon. Sausage."

"Sounds great. Can I do anything to help?"

"If you want to make the coffee, that would be great," she said. "We're almost ready to eat."

Whistling along with the music, Jim moved around the kitchen, making the coffee, while Donna tended to the pans on the stove. It felt natural, like they'd always been like this. As if they'd spent years puttering around the kitchen together, making breakfast.

As Donna served up two plates of food, Jim poured the coffee. Once seated at the kitchen table, they sat down and tucked into their meal.

Jim scooped scrambled eggs into his mouth. He was hungry.

"Does it hurt?" Donna asked, indicating the cut on his forehead.

"Nah, not at all," he said.

They made small talk while they ate their breakfast. They decided they'd like to do Christmas dinner together. Once they settled on the venue—Donna's house—they went over the menu. Jim helped himself to a second stack of pancakes, and Donna poured more coffee.

"I'll have to go see how Sarge is doing," Donna ventured.

"Do you want me to go with you?" Jim asked. Sarge could be spiky and he wanted to spare Donna getting caught in the crosshairs.

Donna shook her head as she added a bit of sugar and creamer to her cup. "No, that's all right. Best to go and get it over with or she'll hold me up in the line at the grocery store for the rest of my life."

"If you change your mind, let me know," he said, dousing his pancakes with maple syrup.

She smiled. "Thanks, I will."

Once breakfast was finished, Jim helped Donna clear the table and load the dishwasher. When all was cleaned up, Donna poured two more cups of coffee and they sat back down at her kitchen table.

"It's time to talk," Jim said.

Donna nodded. "It is, Jim."

Jim looked at Donna and cleared his throat, trying to dislodge the lump that had formed there. "Donna, your letter is something I will cherish for the rest of my life."

She smiled warmly at him. "I meant every word I said. I'm looking forward to going to California with you."

He laughed. "I appreciate that more than you can ever know, but it's not necessary."

Donna's smile disappeared. "You don't want me to go with you?"

Immediately he reached for her hands and took them in his. He spoke quickly to reassure her. "It's what I wanted to tell you last night. I'm going to turn down the job, Donna. I've changed my mind."

"Why?" she asked, her eyes widening.

"Lots of reasons. I just retired from the workforce, so why would I want to go back to that grind? And I've decided I want to spearhead a campaign to build a small homeless shelter here in Orchard Falls."

Donna sat up straighter in her chair. "That's a great idea, Jim. And so needed." She paused and asked, "But are you sure? I don't want to hold you back."

"No, Donna, you would never hold me back. No, I've been thinking about this. I'm staying put. At first, taking the job in California seemed like the answer, but then I realized that the location wasn't the problem. The problem is me getting used to the fact that my military career is behind me. If I left, I'd just be transferring the same set of issues from here to there."

"No matter where you go or where you live, you always take

yourself with you," Donna added. "And that includes all your baggage."

"But most of all, Donna, I can't leave you," Jim said. "Not again. And it makes me love you more, knowing you'd give up Orchard Falls for me, but I won't ask that of you."

"So you're not going to California," Donna said. She sighed and then grinned. "I guess I'll unpack my bikini then, and cancel my order for a surfboard."

Jim burst out laughing.

They were both quiet, each lost in their own thoughts, trying to navigate the turn their lives had taken.

"I'm afraid you're stuck with me." Jim laughed.

Her eyes filled with unshed tears. "I'm happy about that."

"You know, Donna, I've done all the talking and you've hardly said anything," Jim said. "I don't mean to dominate."

Donna laughed out loud. "Oh, Jim, you've been dominating conversations since I met you." Once she stopped laughing, she looked at him with warmth in her eyes. "And I wouldn't have you any other way."

"Whew! That's relief!" Jim joked.

"But I spent a lot of time thinking about things. You. Me. Us. Examining my feelings for you and what it would mean if you were to leave," Donna explained. "We have a second chance at love. I don't want to miss that."

"I feel so lucky to have found you again."

Finally, Donna asked, "Are we exchanging Christmas gifts this year? I know it's short notice."

Jim grinned. "You bet we are. I've already bought yours."

"You have?" Donna asked.

"I have," he said. "This is going to be the best Christmas ever."

CHAPTER 21

he day before Christmas Eve, Donna found herself on the front porch of Sarge and Ralph's house. She could hear the muted sounds of a television coming from the front room. After she rang the doorbell, she waited and looked around the neighborhood, disappointed at the lack of snow, but with all the decorations and lights of the neighboring houses, it remained cheery.

The front door opened, and Ralph broke into smile. "Donna!" He held the storm door wide open so she could enter. She stepped inside and immediately was aware of the immense heat and the ear-piercing volume of the television. Beads of perspiration broke out on her brow. Ralph waved her in to the front parlor. Sarge sat in an easy chair with her leg in a cast elevated on a stool.

"Well, well, look who the wind blew in," Sarge said by way of a greeting. She picked up the remote control to mute the volume and set it back down on the arm of her chair.

"How are you doing?" Donna asked. At Ralph's invitation, she sat down on the sofa. Donna unbuttoned her coat and loosened her scarf, as she was beginning to sweat with the fierce heat.

Sarge folded her arms across her chest. "How do you think I'm doing with a broken leg for Christmas?"

"It's not Donna's fault," said Ralph.

Sarge whipped her head around to her husband. "She told me to break a leg before the race! What kind of voodoo is that?"

Ralph laughed, which Donna thought was brave. Or foolish. "That didn't have anything to do with it."

"Easy for you to say—your leg isn't in a cast," Sarge said.

Before their conversation could escalate or deteriorate, Donna held up her gift bag. "I've brought you some chocolates."

Sarge sighed. "Well, that's something, I suppose."

Donna set the bag down on the coffee table. She looked around the living room, a heavily wallpapered room with sculpted carpeting. There were knickknacks everywhere; every available space was covered with a figurine or something glass or ceramic. Donna thought it must be a nightmare to dust. There was a small Christmas tree on a table in the front window with lights, tinsel, and ornaments.

"What are your plans for Christmas?" Donna asked.

"Not much," Ralph said.

Donna had an idea, and before she could give it too much thought and talk herself out of it, she blurted, "Would you like to come to my house for Christmas dinner?"

"Have you lost your mind, Donna?" Sarge asked. "Christmas dinner is for families."

Feeling courageous, Donna challenged her. "Oh, come on, Sarge, I've known you all my life, and if that doesn't count for something, I don't know what does."

"May I ask what's on the menu?" Ralph said.

"No, you may not," Sarge said firmly. "Who will be there?"

Ralph raised an eyebrow at his wife.

"Just Brent and me, and Jim and Leah," Donna answered.

Sarge's head shot up. "Jim O'Hara? It's about time the two of you got together." She rolled her eyes. "That only took forever."

Even Donna had to laugh, and Sarge looked at her like she thought she was an idiot.

"I won't be able to bring anything," Sarge said. "As you can see, I'm laid up. Some idiot told me to break a leg before the toboggan race."

Donna winced at the memory. She knew Sarge would never let her live this down, but she didn't care. "That's fine. Just bring yourself." She looked over at Sarge's long-suffering husband. "And Ralph, of course."

"What time is dinner?" Sarge asked.

"Four in the afternoon," Donna replied.

"That late?" Sarge asked with a sniff of disapproval.

"Is two better?" Donna asked.

"Yeah, it is," Sarge said. She turned to her husband. "Well, Ralph, what do you think? Will we go to Donna's this year instead of my deadbeat brother's?"

Donna tried not to wince again.

"It's fine by me, Sarge," Ralph said.

"Good. We'll be there, Donna."

Ralph walked Donna to the door.

"Again, I'm so sorry about everything that's happened," Donna said, stepping out onto the front porch. Donna was barely out the door before the volume of the television was back up to its previous setting.

"Don't give it another thought. And pay no attention to Sarge. Her bark has always been worse than her bite." Ralph lowered his voice. "She gets herself all worked up over this toboggan race. I'm telling you, during the run-up to the festival there's no living with her."

Donna was dying to ask how he lived with her the rest of the year, but kept that to herself.

"Are you sure we can't bring a bottle of wine or something?"

Donna shook her head. "Not necessary, Ralph."

"One more thing," Ralph said. He whispered, "What's on the menu?"

Donna laughed.

"I like to think about what's for dinner. It gives me something to look forward to. And there's no bigger dinner than Christmas dinner."

Donna had to agree with him.

"Turkey and ham, mashed potatoes and gravy, stuffing, cranberry sauce, carrots, turnip, corn, Brussels sprouts, rolls, and of course, all sorts of Christmas desserts."

Ralph raised his eyes to heaven. "It sounds wonderful, Donna. I don't really care that Sarge's brother is a deadbeat. That's his business. But his wife is a terrible cook."

ON CHRISTMAS EVE, Donna took extra care getting the house ready for the coming celebration. Since Monday, she and Jim had spent a lot of time together. They'd gone shopping for last-minute gifts and for the dinner they were going to cook together on Christmas Day. Leah had offered to make a few vegan dishes, so there was going to be plenty of food for the six of them.

Snow fell lightly through the afternoon, but it wasn't enough to accumulate, melting as soon as it hit the ground. Donna kept looking out the window and biting her lip, wistful. A white Christmas would be the icing on the cake.

She put some final touches on her Christmas tree with some last-minute ornaments she'd picked up at the Snowball Festival. She arranged some cheery-looking poinsettias in their red-foiled pots on the bay window. She turned on all her Christmas lights inside and out, and they would remain turned on until she went to bed Christmas night. The Carpenters' *Christmas Portrait* played on the record player. It was nostalgic for Donna because it was the first album she'd bought as a kid at Christmastime.

Jim had put the extra leaf in her dining-room table and had picked up her Christmas tablecloth from the dry cleaners, where she'd dropped it off to have it professionally pressed.

She made herself some hot chocolate and sat down on her sofa, taking a break to reflect and enjoy the day. As she'd grown older, Christmas had meant different things. Like life, it was cyclic. When she was a kid, it was all about the presents under the tree. Her favorite gift still remained Baby Alive when she was eight. In high school, it was all about trendy clothes and albums under the tree. When she was dating Jim, those Christmases had been magical. Then when she married and had Brent, Christmas and its meaning took on a whole new dimension. It became no longer about her but about other people. Her husband, her parents, his parents, and mostly, Brent. She took on the preparing of Christmas dinner and loved having family at her house, around her table. But the best Christmases were the ones when Brent was little and believed in Santa Claus. Playing Santa Claus had been one of the best times of her life. She thought of her late husband and raised her cup to him. He'd been a good husband and father. The two of them used to take the day off and do all the Christmas shopping in one day. Those had been happy times. But Christmases these past few years, especially since Brent moved out, had been more sedate. This year, Donna was excited about the addition of Jim and Leah. She and Brent had doubled their numbers. And with Sarge and Ralph, it would be even more festive.

Donna's thoughts were interrupted by the phone ringing.

It was Jim.

"Hey there, how are you?" Donna asked, smiling, feeling satisfied and content.

"I'm good," Jim said. "I want to run something by you."

"Sure."

"I'm at the hardware store. Mr. Brenneman just mentioned to me that he's not going to his sister's for Christmas, because she's gone into the hospital."

"Would he like to come here for dinner?" Donna asked.

"That's what I was thinking, but I wanted to ask you first," Jim said.

"Please invite him."

"I will. See you later. Do you need anything from the store?" he asked.

"No, we're all set."

"Okay, see you in a bit."

"And Jim—"

"Yes?" he said.

"There was no need to ask. You could have just invited Mr. Brenneman."

Jim went quiet. "Thank you, Donna."

She was just about to hang up when Jim said, "Donna—"

"Yes?"

He laughed. "The Christmas lights came in Monday morning."

She could practically see him grinning on the other end of the line.

"That figures," she said, and she started laughing, too.

THE AIR WAS crisp and dry when the four of them left for church, half an hour before midnight. Because the roads and sidewalks were clear, the four of them had decided to walk. Brent and Leah walked ahead of Donna and Jim. Donna wore an ivory-colored winter coat with a beret and scarf in emerald green. Jim wore a black overcoat over his suit.

When they crossed the first block, Jim reached for Donna's hand. She smiled at him, happier than she'd been in a long time. Up ahead, the chattering between Brent and Leah floated along in the air, punctuated by giggling and laughter. The words weren't discernable, but the sense was one of merriment.

As they rounded the corner onto Main Street, they were joined by small crowds of people heading to church. There was a general feeling of anticipation in the air. The conversations were hushed but excited. All the shops were closed but their windows were lit up with Christmas lights. Traffic on the road was minimal, and Donna gasped when they arrived at the church.

The front doors of the church were wide open. The choir was rehearsing and their voices drifted out into the cold, starry night. Before entering the church, Donna glanced up at the sky for any signs of snow.

Inside, lit candles flickered along the base of the windows. Ushers handed out tapers with paper sleeves as churchgoers entered. The church was packed. Donna looked around for seats for the four of them, but all the pews appeared full.

"We may have to split up," Jim said, reading her mind.

"There's two seats over there," Brent said, pointing. He looked at Jim. "Mom and Leah can sit there and we can stand at the back." There was a group of men already standing at the back, some of them leaning against the wall.

Jim nodded. "Okay ladies, we'll see you after the service."

Although Donna was disappointed over the fact that the four of them wouldn't be able to sit together, she was glad to be sharing the pew with Leah. She told herself to remember next year to leave the house a few minutes earlier.

The candlelit midnight service never failed to bring tears to Donna's eyes. The choir was well-tuned and by the time it was over, Donna felt uplifted and was looking forward to celebrating Christmas with those she loved.

Leah turned to her in the pew. "That was really beautiful." Her blue eyes blazed and she wore her blonde hair in an updo. She was a kind person, Donna thought, and her devotion to animals was commendable. Her bubbly personality complemented Brent's quieter one. Donna felt Leah was a good match for her son.

"It was, wasn't it?" Donna said, smiling at her. One of the things she was looking forward to in the New Year was getting to know Leah better.

They filed out of the pew with the rest of the churchgoers and joined Jim and Brent, who waited for them at the back of the church.

With his hand on the small of her back, Jim escorted Donna out of the church. When Donna stepped outside, she let out a squeal of delight.

"Look, it's snowing!"

Everyone looked up. Big, heavy snowflakes fell rapidly.

"Looks like you'll get your white Christmas, Donna." Jim smiled.

"Mom, will I go home and get the car and come back for you two?" Brent asked.

She felt Jim stiffen beside her. She squeezed Jim's hand and whispered, "He's just being thoughtful."

"I'm not that old," Jim protested in a whisper.

Donna laughed. "No, you're not."

"Mom?" Brent called.

"We prefer to walk, honey," Donna said.

"But thanks, all the same," Jim added.

"We'll catch up with you back at the house," Brent said.

Donna waved them off. "They're young. They probably want to be alone."

"I'm not so young anymore, and I want to be alone with you," Jim said, taking her hand in his.

Donna smiled. Why did it feel like she and Jim had always

been together? She was excited about this next chapter in her life with him.

"Will we walk to the end of Main Street? Enjoy the moment?" Jim asked.

"I'd love that."

They walked arm in arm. The snow had picked up and swirled around them. Snowflakes stuck to their coats and to Jim's hair. They waved goodbye to other people and wished everyone they passed a Merry Christmas.

They arrived at the statue of Horace. He still sported his knitted scarf. The town hall lights illuminated the falling snow. They stood in front of the statue and looked down Main Street, the snow falling and accumulating on the street amidst the yellows, greens, reds, and blues of Christmas lights. Giant red ornaments hung from the old-fashioned streetlights. "It looks so beautiful," Donna said, her voice catching.

"You look beautiful, Donna," Jim said softly. They faced each other in front of Horace as the snow fell heavily around them.

"Jim . . ."

"Donna, you still owe me one kiss for Christmas," Jim said. Donna smiled. "Just one?"

Jim laughed. "Well, maybe more than one."

He took Donna in his arms and pulled her close. His embrace was warm, and Donna thought she could stay there forever. When he leaned down toward her, Donna parted her lips slightly in anticipation. Her heart raced.

"Merry Christmas, Donna," Jim whispered. His lips were warm and firm, and Donna yielded to his kiss. She shivered but not from the cold. She let herself get carried away in his kiss.

Him kissing her wasn't as Donna remembered it used to be. It was so much better. Donna felt like she had come home. To that place where happy memories are made, where one feels safe, and most of all, where one feels loved.

EPILOGUE

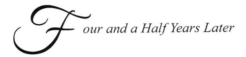
Four and a Half Years Later

DONNA RETURNED from her yoga class and laid her bag on the table in her new kitchen. She and Jim had sold their houses and purchased this one together, two blocks away from their old homes, when they started their life together after marrying three years ago.

There was the buzz of the lawn mower outside. From the window, she saw Jim cutting the grass in the backyard.

They had a big evening planned. The official opening of the homeless shelter was scheduled for later that evening. Donna was so proud of Jim. Singlehandedly, he had spearheaded a campaign to get a purpose-built shelter in Orchard Falls. There had been endless fundraisers, pledges, and good old-fashioned door-to-door canvassing. The town had rallied behind him. Even Sarge and Ralph had been enthusiastic about the venture and had come up with the idea of a food pantry within the shelter.

The building had unofficially opened two weeks ago. It was

impressive. Jim had managed to secure a site within walking distance of the underpass. There were beds and showers and food. The food pantry accepted donations of canned and dried goods.

Jim had been asked to run it but he declined, telling the board he was enjoying retirement too much with his wife. But they made him an honorary member of the board anyway, and he continued to volunteer at both the shelter and the soup table.

Donna listened, tilting her head. The lawnmower had ceased. Humming a tune, she pulled a tub of candy cane ice cream from the bottom of the freezer. She'd purchased it after Christmas before they pulled it off the shelf, and had hid it in the bottom drawer of the freezer. She knew Jim would never find it back there. The mercury was well over ninety degrees, and if ever there was a time for ice cream, it was now.

From the window over the sink, she watched as he sat down on the bench of the glider swing. She had just the thing for him. She grabbed two spoons from the drawer and carried them and the ice cream outside.

He smiled when he saw her approaching and patted the empty space beside him.

She held up the carton of ice cream and the two spoons.

As she neared, an expression of surprise spread across his face. She never tired of looking at him. As she had suspected, the scar from the stitches did not detract from his handsomeness.

"Is that candy cane ice cream?" he asked with a grin.

She sat down next to him and handed him a spoon. She peeled off the lid and laid it on the bench beside her. Her wedding ring, a band of diamonds and emeralds, glittered in the afternoon sun.

"Where did you get this?" he asked.

She smiled at him with a raised eyebrow. "I have my resources."

"What time are Leah and Brent bringing the baby over tomorrow?" Jim asked.

"After breakfast," she said. Brent and Leah were going off for a long weekend to a conference on animal rights. And Donna and Jim were babysitting their granddaughter, Hannah. "I'm so excited, I can't wait."

"I know you are, Grandma O'Hara. I am, too." Jim threw his arm around her shoulder, pulled her close and kissed her forehead.

Donna glanced at her wedding band and then over at Jim. "I'm happy, Jim."

Jim looked at her and smiled, his face reflecting how she felt. "Me, too." He kissed her again, this time on the lips. That one kiss at Christmas had turned into a million kisses, and Donna never tired of them.

Jim took his spoon, scooped out some ice cream, and put it into his mouth. "That's great stuff."

Donna licked her own spoon. "It sure is."

"Here's to Christmas in July," Jim said, and they clinked their spoons together.

ALSO BY MICHELE BROUDER

The Happy Holiday Series

A Whyte Christmas

This Christmas

A Wish for Christmas

The Happy Holidays Box Set Books 1-3

The Escape to Ireland Series

A Match Made in Ireland

Her Fake, Irish Husband

Her Irish Inheritance

Soul Saver Series

Claire Daly: Reluctant Soul Saver

Claire Daly: Marked for Collection

WEBSITE

If you find any typos or other problems, please let me know. As hard as we try, a few typos always manage to slip through. I'd love to hear from you. Feel free to reach out to me at michele@michelebrouder.com

Visit my website and sign up for my newsletter at www.michelebrouder.com to get bonus material exclusive to newsletter subscribers only as well as news about upcoming releases and other fun things. I hate spam just as much as you and you can be assured that your email address will never be passed on to a third party.

Warm Regards,
Michele Brouder

ABOUT THE AUTHOR

Michele Brouder is originally from the Buffalo, New York area. She has lived in the southwest of Ireland since 2006, except for a two-year stint in Florida. She makes her home with her husband, two boys, and a dog named Rover. Her go to place is, was, and will always be the beach. Any beach. Any weather.

Printed in Great Britain
by Amazon